D0402647

Moon at Nine

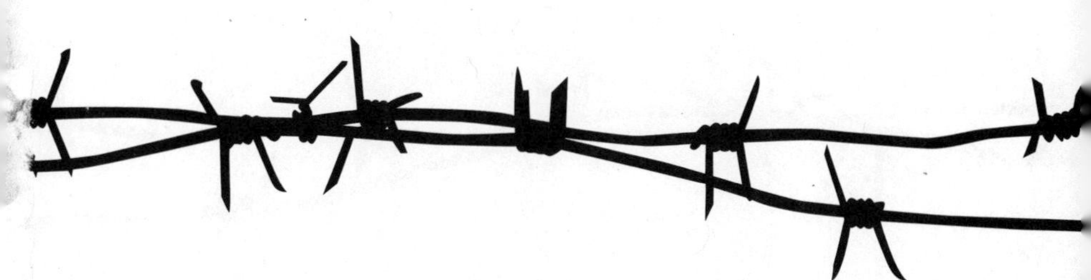

Moon at Nine

DEBORAH ELLIS

First published in the United States in 2014

This is a first edition.
10 9 8 7 6 5 4 3 2 1

www.pajamapress.ca info@pajamapress.ca

The publisher gratefully acknowledges the support of the Canada Council for the Arts and the Ontario Arts Council for its publishing program. We acknowledge the financial support of the Government of Canada through the Book Publishing Industry Development Program (BPIDP) for our publishing activities.

Library and Archives Canada Cataloguing in Publication

Ellis, Deborah, 1960-, author

Moon at nine / Deborah Ellis.

ISBN 978-1-927485-57-6 (bound).

1. Iran--Social conditions--1979-1997--Juvenile fiction. I. Title.

PS8559.L5494M66 2014 jC813'.54 C2013-907300-0

Publisher Cataloging-in-Publication Data (U.S.)

Ellis, Deborah, 1960-
Moon at nine / Deborah Ellis.
[224] pages : cm.
Summary: Fifteen-year-old Farrin has grown up with secrets: ten years after the overthrow of the Shah, her aristocratic mother is still working against Iran's conservative revolutionary government. But when Farrin befriends Sadira, the intriguing and outgoing new student at her school for gifted girls, her own new secret is even more dangerous. Because the girls discover their relationship is more than just a friendship—and in Iran, being gay is punishable by death.

ISBN-13: 978-1-927485-57-6

1. Lesbians – Juvenile fiction. 2. Iran – History, 1997 – Juvenile fiction. I. Title.

[Fic] dc23 PZ7.E554Mo 2014

Cover design: Rebecca Buchanan
Interior page design: Rebecca Buchanan and Martin Gould
Image credits: iStockphoto/©elmira (skyline of Tehran), Shutterstock/©Aleksandar Mijatovic (woman), Shutterstock/©Dundanim (moon), Shutterstock/©oriontrail (starry sky), Shutterstock/©Talashow (barbed wire). Author photo courtesy of John Spray.

Manufactured by Friesens in Altona, Manitoba, Canada in 2014.

Pajama Press Inc.
112 Berkeley St., Toronto, Ontario Canada, M5A 2W7
www.pajamapress.ca

Distributed in the US by Orca Book Publishers
PO Box 468 Custer, WA, 98240-0468, USA

To those who have loved and have perished for it,
and to those who love still,
dancing and rejoicing in the face of oppression.

I'm the keeper of my secrets, aware of my time.

Hafez

Part One

This novel is based on a true story.

One
1988

DEMON HUNTERS OF THE DESERT

Ancient demons roam an ancient land.

They dwell in the valleys and lurk in the mountains. They hide among the grains of sand and sleep beside the scorpions.

They watch the humans go on about their insignificant business—shopping in the markets, heeding the call to prayer, taking care of their children. The humans are busy. The demons go unnoticed.

The demons play their games and inflict their pain—a train crash here, a sick child there—and the humans blame themselves, their own failings, beating their chests and decrying their weaknesses before God.

The demons just laugh.

And thus the eons pass.

Until one of the humans finally wakes up, opens her eyes, and decides to fight back.

"You're writing about demons."

Principal Kobra's voice was hard and humorless.

Farrin lifted her eyes from her open notebook on the principal's desk and looked into the woman's face. She tried to figure out how much trouble she was in.

"She was supposed to be doing chemistry." This came from the third person in the office. Pargol, the class monitor, was one of the most powerful students in the school. She was also the biggest rat.

"My assignment was completed," Farrin said. "I wrote this after my work was done."

"So you know all there is to know about chemistry, then," Principal Kobra said. "How lucky we are to have such a brilliant student at our school. What is the chemical formula for carbon tetrachloride?"

Farrin knew the answer and fired it back, only to have another question thrown at her, then another and another. When she finally stumbled, Pargol answered in her place. Farrin wanted to slap the smirk right off the monitor's face.

"Stop slouching!"

The order took Farrin by surprise. She didn't respond right away.

"Stand up straight!"

Farrin was already standing as straight as she thought any human could, but she lifted her head and shifted her body slightly to make it look like she was obeying. Now, instead of looking at the face of the principal, she was staring straight into the eyes of Ayatollah Khomeini. A large portrait of the

Iranian leader hung on the wall over the principal's desk, just as it hung in every room in the school.

The principal was just getting warmed up.

"Do you think we fought for the revolution and kicked the Shah out of power just so you could stand there and slouch?"

"No, Principal Kobra."

"So many Iranians died in the bombing last night, and so many more will likely die tonight, and you stand there and slouch. It's obscene."

"I'm sorry, Principal Kobra."

"Perhaps you think you know more than your teacher," the principal said. "Your chemistry teacher has a Master of Science degree, but you know better. Perhaps you think you know better than your class monitor. Pargol comes from a family that has given three sons to the war with Iraq. She is the highest achieving student in your year, while you lag behind in fifteenth position, but you know better."

There was a rumor around school that in her free time, just for fun, Principal Kobra was an interrogator at Evin Prison.

"No, Principal Kobra."

Principal Kobra picked up Farrin's notebook and held it in her hand.

"You are writing about demons," she said again. "Demons in the desert." She flipped through the pages of the notebook, stopping here and there to read a phrase or examine a drawing. Farrin held her breath—there were sketches of the principal in that notebook.

"Are these demons supposed to be in Iran?"

"Yes, Principal Kobra."

"You want to be careful not to perpetuate a stereotype," the principal said. "Iran is only thirty percent desert. It is also mountains and marshes and lakes and fertile regions and cities."

"Yes, Principal Kobra. I mean to put all those into the story," Farrin said. "The inspiration was the *shahnameh*, where the hero battles dragons."

That was a lie, of course. Farrin's inspiration for the story was a grainy VHS recording of an old American television show, *Kolchak: The Night Stalker*, brought in secret to Farrin's house by the Briefcase Man. But she wasn't about to say that!

"You aspire to be another Ferdowsi?" asked the principal, speaking with reverence the name of one of Iran's ancient storytellers. "An admirable goal."

"Thank you, Principal Kobra." Farrin glanced over at Pargol, who was looking slightly disturbed by this unexpected bit of praise.

"Who do the demons represent?"

In an instant, Farrin saw the smirk return to Pargol's face and realized she'd been asked a question she had no idea how to answer. Which meant it was a dangerous question. In Iran, it was important to always be prepared with answers. It was best if the answers were true. At the very least, the answers had to be believable and on the right side of politics.

Who were the demons? In Farrin's mind, they were just demons—standard, run-of-the-mill creatures of the underworld and the afterlife, djinn and ghouls, shape-shifters and blood-sucking foot-lickers. She was writing the story because she saw an episode of *The Night Stalker* that had a Middle Eastern demon in it, and the show had gotten it all wrong. But that answer would not do.

"Who do they represent?" Farrin repeated the question to give herself time to think.

"That's not a difficult question," the principal said, "for a smart girl like you. You are fifteen, not five. Surely you don't believe that fairies and pixies really exist. I know you've studied allegory in your literature classes. So I'll ask you again and I want an answer straight away or I'll have to start wondering if you are hiding something. Who do the demons represent?"

Farrin's parents were always warning her to keep her mouth shut and her activities beyond question. "They're watching us," her mother said. "We're trying to put the Shah back in power. Nothing is more important than that. So behave yourself. All it takes is one mistake."

She had a sudden flash of brilliance. She actually grinned as she said, "The demons represent the antirevolutionary forces, Principal Kobra!"

Principal Kobra stood up and came around her desk to stand a few short feet in front of Farrin.

"Apologize to your class monitor for forcing her to report you."

Farrin turned to Pargol and said in a voice that sounded as sincere as she could manage, "I'm sorry."

"And?" the principal asked.

"And...thank you for helping me become a better student." Farrin knew what was expected. She'd deal later with that rat of a monitor.

"I suppose you want this back," the principal said, holding up the notebook. "Do I need to remind you that this is a school for gifted girls? You have been invited into it, and you can also be invited out. Writing stories about demons during class time is an insult to your chemistry teacher. If you don't want to pay attention to your studies, we can find someone else to sit at your desk."

Principal Kobra held the notebook out to Farrin but kept a firm grip on it.

"You are a smart girl, Farrin," the principal added in a quiet voice. "You are strong willed and you are smart. These are good qualities. These are qualities all Iranian women should have. These are qualities that give you confidence. Just be careful you don't end up with too much confidence."

She released her hand from Farrin's notebook and nodded her dismissal.

Farrin retreated as fast as her legs would take her. She wasn't worried about maintaining any shreds of dignity. All she wanted was to escape.

Two

Farrin plotted her revenge all the way to the cloakroom.

She was so tired of that sneak monitor sticking her nose into everybody's business. School would be fine without Pargol and her spies. Farrin could parrot back the right answers in her revolution classes. Most of her teachers were enthusiastic about their subjects and really cared that their students learned. And even though Farrin had no friends at the school, she had to admit that most of the students were all right, despite what her mother said about them belonging to the wrong social class. She might even enjoy herself if she were able to have one or two friends there.

"If you want friends, I will find you friends," was one of her mother's standard phrases. "We can't allow you to become involved with some low-class rabble. When I was a girl, that school was really a special place—"

And Mom would be off on one of her good-old-days tirades. She had attended Farrin's school back when it was a place where moneyed families sent their daughters to be "finished" rather than educated. After the revolution, it was turned into a school for intelligent girls from all over Tehran. Admission was by test score only, and tuition was free. Girls from all sorts of families attended now.

"It's not the same," Farrin's mother would whine. She refused to go to prize-giving ceremonies, even when her daughter received a prize. "There's no value in distinguishing yourself among a pack of dirt-dwellers," was another of her mother's sayings. "Do your work to avoid trouble, but there is nothing to be gained by flaunting it and drawing attention to yourself. There's too much at stake."

It was like a crazy balancing act. Farrin had to do her work well enough to avoid getting kicked out—since whatever other school she'd have to go to would be worse—but she could never become engaged enough to attract notice. As a result, she was often sent home with *could-do-betters* on her report card.

Farrin didn't care about that. Her whole life was about living with lies.

She was five when the Shah of Iran was overthrown by what her mother called the dirt-dwelling rabble. Everything changed. Women had to cover their heads—not one single strand of hair could show or the Revolutionary Guards would harass them, right on the street. There were women in the Guards whose job it was to drive around the city and look for women who were not dressed according to the new rules.

"There's a career for you," her mother would sneer whenever they'd been stopped and yelled at for a clothing violation. "All the things that need fixing in this country and they worry about *hair*." Her mother would mutter almost under her breath. On the streets the spies could be anywhere, just as it was at Farrin's school. Farrin grew up wearing two faces—one face she wore when she was out in the world and another face she wore when she was in private.

The story she was writing in her notebook was an attempt to escape all that. It had nothing to do with politics, nothing to do with the Shah, nothing to do with the revolution, nothing to do with religion. Just an exciting story about a girl battling demons and winning.

Farrin stomped through the halls, past the giant revolutionary slogans on the walls, barely noticing the white-chadored younger girls scurrying to get out of her way. She clutched her notebook so tightly that the wire coils were imprinted on the palm of her hand.

The story might have been really good, good enough to be made into a book. And maybe the book would have been so good and so popular that it would have been made into a TV show, a TV show that might have been shown around the world, and then everyone would know that Iran had strong, clever, creative girls...and maybe she'd have been invited to make other TV shows in England or even in America.

Now it was all ruined. All because of that horrible Pargol.

Pargol would have to pay.

Farrin turned into the cloakroom. Rows of black chadors hung from pegs.

The school uniform was a black tunic with a gray headscarf for the older girls and a white scarf for the juniors. Most of the girls wore long, dark gray manteaus outside. The ones from the most conservative families, which included all the monitors, wore voluminous black chadors over their school clothes.

Farrin wore the manteau. Her mother considered the chador a symbol of the revolution, and therefore something that was against the Shah.

Farrin plopped down on the bench beneath her peg. Each student had a peg on the wall, a spot on a bench, and a crate underneath for things like outdoor shoes and sports equipment. Farrin threw her notebook to the floor by her crate.

All that work! All those dreams! She felt silly now, like some little kid who still believed in fairy tales.

She stared at her notebook; it had landed in a pod of dust. The girls in charge of cleaning the cloakroom that week hadn't done their job very well. There was rubbish all around.

Rubbish, Farrin thought. *That's all my demon story is.*

Her eyes landed on a nib of white chalk, lying in the gray dust like a tiny mushroom in the forest. It was an unusual bit of rubbish. The teachers jealously guarded school supplies, since there were never enough of them to go around. A piece of chalk, adrift and ownerless, was unheard of.

Farrin looked around. All the other students were at one of the mandatory after-school enrichment activities. She was alone in the cloakroom. In a flash, she bent down and picked up the chalk. The black chadors looked an awful lot like chalkboards.

Trembling all over—since what she was doing was definitely breaking the rules—Farrin found Pargol's chador, spread it out so that she had a flat surface to work on, and made her first chalk mark. The white chalk stood out starkly against the black cloth.

Then she hesitated. What to write? She didn't want Pargol to get arrested, just yelled at by woman from the Revolutionary Guard.

Her imagination failed her. Worried that someone would come into the cloakroom and catch her, she quickly drew a large white circle, put two dots inside it for eyes, and added a big, grinning semicircle for a mouth. Then she pocketed the chalk and sat back down by her own peg. She opened up her crate just as a flood of chattering juniors opened the cloakroom door and streamed inside.

Farrin leaned against the wall. The younger girls always looked so happy, so unconcerned. Did they have any worries? Had she been like that when she was younger? Were any of them covering up their parents' secrets, like she was? She admired their easy way with each other—the chatting, the joking, the giggling, the jostling. They were like mice.

No burdens, Farrin thought. *They can't possibly be carrying any burdens.*

The door opened again for more juniors. Through the cacophony of conversation, Farrin heard a different sound. It was a sound she had never heard before at that school, and it was so unexpected that for a moment she had trouble identifying it.

But then she knew.

It was music.

Music itself was not against the law in Iran. Songs about the revolution were encouraged. But any other music had not been allowed officially as far back as Farrin could remember.

The sound disappeared with the closing of the door then could be heard again as a few juniors grabbed their backpacks and left the cloakroom to start their journeys home.

Straining to hear, Farrin grew frustrated.

"All of you, shut up!" she ordered.

Shocked, the other juniors went quiet for a moment, then one of the little rodents piped up, "It's just Farrin. No one cares about her." To Farrin, the junior added, "You're not a monitor. We don't have to obey you."

"You've been alive for just five minutes," Farrin shot back. "You know nothing, so shut up."

In the bit of quiet they gave her, she heard the notes again.

"It's called music," the rodent said. Farrin stalked out of the cloakroom with the laughter of the juniors nipping at her heels.

Farrin followed the sound of the music a short way down the hall and around the corner. The supply closet door was slightly open. The music was coming from inside.

She was about to push open the door to see who was doing this forbidden thing when she stopped. She couldn't bring herself to interrupt just yet; she wanted the music to keep going.

The tune was being played on a santour, an Iranian instrument with many strings. It was a classical piece. She recognized it from the records her parents occasionally played in secret—one of the many forbidden things they did.

The tune was played so beautifully, so perfectly, that Farrin wondered if it was a recording. She had to know. She opened the door wide enough to peer in.

A student was playing, a girl from the senior school, judging by the color of her head covering. Farrin couldn't see who it was. Light from the bare bulb that hung from the ceiling cast a shadow across the student's face. If the girl noticed that someone was watching her, she gave no sign. The music went on seamlessly.

Farrin watched and listened, transfixed by the sounds. The school disappeared, Pargol disappeared, everything disappeared but the notes that entered her like rays of pure moonlight.

She closed her eyes and let the music draw her in.

Then it ended and she was back in the doorway.

"Looking for something?"

Farrin opened her eyes. The student musician raised her head.

Farrin felt something like a jolt of electricity through her body as the most intense green eyes looked right into hers.

For a moment, Farrin forgot how to breathe. "Yes, I need...no, I mean...you can't play that."

"I'm not very good yet," the musician said.

"No, no, you're great, but you can't...I mean, it's forbidden. You'll get into trouble."

"If it's *really* forbidden, the school wouldn't have a santour," the girl said. "I think the rule against music is more of a suggestion than a rule. That's what I choose to think, anyway." She played a final little tune then packed away the little mallets used to strike the strings. She covered the santour with a cloth and put it away on a shelf. "I wandered in here by accident—I thought it was the door to a classroom—and when I saw the santour I couldn't resist."

"I won't tell anyone," Farrin promised.

"Thank you," the girl said, with a radiant smile. "But don't carry the burden of a secret because of me. Do you play?"

"The santour?" Farrin asked. There was no good answer to that sort of question. If she admitted that she played piano—although not nearly so well as this girl played the santour—then she'd be admitting to doing something forbidden herself. She didn't know if this girl was a rat or not. Farrin decided not to answer. Instead, she said, "You thought the closet was a classroom."

"Today is my first day," the girl replied. "My name is Sadira."

Sadira. Farrin silently repeated the name to herself. It was a beautiful name.

The girl looked at her with amusement, as if she was waiting for something. Farrin couldn't figure out what she was waiting for.

The sound of yelling intruded on them.

"What's that?" Sadira asked, pushing the door open farther and standing next to Farrin in the doorway. Farrin caught a scent of jasmine.

"That's just Pargol, one of the monitors, screaming at the juniors," Farrin said. Pargol must have found the chalk drawing on her chador.

"That's not right," Sadira said. She left Farrin behind at the closet door and headed toward the classroom. Farrin scurried after her, anxious to keep the other girl out of trouble.

"Pargol yells. That's what she does," Farrin said.

Sadira didn't respond. In quick strides she was at the cloakroom, Farrin right behind her.

Pargol was holding up the chalk-marked chador and bawling out some crying juniors.

"I'll run the whole lot of you up to the principal's office if you don't fess up," Pargol spat out. "You think you can make a fool out of me? Who did this?"

"Oh, is that *your* chador?" Sadira asked, calmly stepping forward. "It seems I made a mistake. I thought I was drawing on my own chador."

"Who are you?" growled Pargol.

"Forgive me," Sadira said, taking the marked-up chador out of Pargol's hands. "I'll just sponge this off for you. Won't take a moment."

She took it over to the sink and used a damp cloth to wipe the chalk away.

"You think that will be the end of it?" Pargol challenged. "You can't just do whatever you want here. I'm a monitor!"

"My name is Sadira," the girl said, handing the clean chador back to Pargol.

Pargol scowled. "You're coming with me to the principal's office."

"Principal Kobra? I met her this morning. She seems very nice."

"She won't be after she finds out what you did."

"What did I do?"

"You drew horrible pictures all over my chador."

"Did I?" Sadira asked, giving Farrin a quick wink.

"I didn't see any drawings," Farrin said.

"You shut up!" said Pargol.

"I didn't see any drawings!" the juniors all said too.

Pargol realized she'd been had.

"Are you *her* friend?" she asked Sadira, jerking her head toward Farrin.

Sadira smiled. "Can't have too many friends," she said mildly.

"You have made your choice, then," Pargol said. "Welcome to *my* territory."

"I'm happy to be here."

"You won't be for long," Pargol said. She yelled at some juniors to get out of her way and stomped out of the cloakroom.

Farrin put on her manteau while Sadira put on her chador. They walked out of the school building together.

"I guess *that* friendship isn't going to work out," Sadira said. "I've been worried about making friends here. Principal Kobra suggested I get to know Pargol."

"Pargol is one of the favorites," Farrin said. "She's one of what Principal Kobra calls the Future Leaders of the World."

"That's a scary thought," Sadira said. "I'd like to believe that future leaders will be better than the ones we have now. Sometimes it seems as if the whole world is run by demons."

Farrin stopped in her tracks. "What did you say?"

Sadira laughed, took Farrin's arm, and led her to the side of the pathway—they were blocking other students who were heading home.

"I didn't mean that I really think the world is ruled by actual demons," Sadira said, "although some of the photos of President Reagan make him look like the Great Satan he's supposed to be! I just think we could do better. Pargol seems like the same old thing, yelling at smaller people to make herself look bigger."

Sadira sat down on a bench in the school yard. Farrin wondered if she should wait to be invited to sit down too—she had no experience of easily hanging out with anyone. Then she felt awkward standing and she sat down beside Sadira on the bench.

Sadira seemed to take that as normal behavior.

So that's how it's done, Farrin thought.

"Can I ask you something?" Sadira asked. "I feel funny asking it, because I'm sure I'm wrong, but it's going to bother me until I know for sure."

She's found out about me, Farrin thought, feeling suddenly cold. She's found out that my mother likes the Shah and no one likes me.

"Go ahead," Farrin said, defeated.

"Does the principal always carry a gun?"

Farrin laughed out loud. "She showed you her pistol? She usually only shows it to students who misbehave. You should hear the juniors cry when they get sent to her office! But she's never shot anybody. No students, anyway."

"She didn't wave it in my face. I just thought I saw it strapped around her waist in a holster. But I wasn't sure."

"She's tough," Farrin said. "Really tough, not just yelling-tough like Pargol. Kobra's got an advanced degree from the women's university in Qom, and she was with the students who took over the American Embassy just after the revolution. I try to stay out of her way."

Sadira took two caramels out of her pocket and handed one to Farrin. "I think I'm going to like it here."

"What was your last school like?"

"I've been out of school for a while," Sadira said, "looking after my father. The rest of my family was killed in a bombing a few years ago—my mom, my brothers, my father's parents who were living with us. They all died."

She said it almost casually. Farrin looked at her in disbelief.

"I have to think about it almost with two brains," Sadira said. "Most of the time, I think of it as a story that happened to someone else. Then I don't really feel it. Do you think that's bad?"

Farrin knew that she was being asked an important question. No one had ever asked her an important question before.

"I think that the people you lost would want you to live," she said.

Sadira nodded. "That's what I think too. Anyway, my father was sick for a long time. He was too sad to look after himself. I stayed home and took care of things and studied on my own. He's feeling better now, so I took the entrance exam for this school and they let me in."

They enjoyed their caramels and watched the stream of students heading across the yard.

I should tell her something about myself, Farrin thought. *It should be something big. She's told me big things about herself. What should I say? That my mother likes the Shah? That I write about demons?"*

Farrin's brain rolled around and around in her cranium, refusing to stop and let a coherent thought come out of her mouth.

This is crazy, Farrin thought. *Just talk to her!*

She was about to blurt out something—anything—when Sadira said, "Oh, here comes my bus!"

Sadira jumped off the bench and hurried to the bus stop.

"I go south," Sadira said, turning around to look at Farrin. "How about you?

"North," said Farrin.

"So, are you going to tell me, or is it a big secret?"

"Tell you what?"

Sadira laughed and took a few steps before turning back and calling, "Your name, silly!"

"Farrin," Farrin told her.

"Farrin," Sadira repeated. "I'll see you tomorrow, Farrin."

Farrin watched Sadira walk away and melt into the crowd of black-chadored schoolgirls rushing to catch the bus.

"She'd make a good demon hunter," Farrin whispered.

THREE

Farrin didn't take a bus home. Her father always sent his car.

"I'm paying the driver anyway," he would say. "He might as well earn his pay."

"If I am driven everywhere, how will I learn my way around the city?" Farrin would say. "You're treating me like a child."

"We're concerned for your safety," her mother would declare.

Three lies, Farrin thought as she crossed the yard to the street where the driver always parked.

Lie number one was that her father paid the driver, a thin, hollow-eyed, middle-aged man named Ahmad. He was an Afghan, one of the millions of refugees in Iran and one of the many employed by Farrin's father. Ahmad worked for food and a mat on the floor of the little stone room by the gate. Her father built his construction empire with nearly free Afghan labor. His workers slept right out at the work sites, which saved her father the cost of hiring security guards. With no other place to sleep, the workers lay in heaps of rags spread out on dirt or on the hard cement. If they asked for a raise, Farrin's father had them deported.

Farrin had even seen him do it once. They'd had a gardener who asked for a salary so he could send the money back to his family in Afghanistan, to help them escape the war. Her father smiled, told the gardener to take a seat, then called one of the buddies he'd bribed in the police force. He was still smiling when the police took the gardener away. He made sure that as many of his workers as possible saw their coworker taken.

Lie number two was that Farrin wanted to take the bus home so she could get to know the city. Her real reason was that she wanted—and some days desperately needed—a break from the adults who had control over her life. Going directly from school to her house made her feel like she was in a cage. If she took a bus, she could get off at a different corner, look in some shops, eat some pizza, or just sit and think her own thoughts.

Lie number three was that her mother was concerned for her safety. "Mom is more concerned about how I look than she is about my safety," Farrin often muttered when she saw Ahmad sitting in the car after school, particularly when it was a fine day with air that had a taste of freedom to it. Her mother only cared about what the ladies in the neighborhood would say if they saw Farrin riding the bus with "the rabble."

After watching Sadira climb into a bus, Farrin felt even more resentful than usual. If Ahmed wasn't waiting, she could have gotten on the bus too. So what if it was going in the wrong direction? She and Sadira could have talked more. She had a feeling this new girl had things to say. And maybe she could have left the bus with Sadira, and maybe walked with her to her house, just to see where she lived. That's what friends did, according to the smuggled American television shows she watched.

Farrin spied her father's car, right where it was supposed to be. The sides and roof had been polished so they glowed, and the chrome sparkled in the sun. Ahmad must have had a slow day. If he wasn't busy, he washed and polished the car so that he would look efficient. He worked hard for his plate of rice and his hard bed.

Ahmad spotted her and hopped out of the car. He opened the door to the backseat and held it open for her.

"Rich girl," one of the students sneered at her as she passed by with a group of giggling friends.

In America, if they called you rich, it would be considered a compliment, Farrin's mother would say if she told her about it. Only in Iran would it be an insult to be called rich! Not just Iran, Farrin knew. In Cuba and in other countries too. She'd learned a few things in her revolution class. But she never argued with her mother about that. Doing so would be like slipping down a black hole of shrill, shrieking tirades.

Farrin leaned against a lamppost, next to the torn remnants of an illegal women's rights poster. She looked across the street at Ahmad. He stood ramrod straight beside the car in his bright white shirt and dark trousers, the closest thing her mother could find to a chauffeur's uniform. He looked puzzled that she was standing and staring instead of crossing the road and getting into the car. But he did not wave or call to her or make any gesture that showed he was impatient.

He's afraid of losing his job, Farrin thought. But that wasn't her problem. Her problem was how to find a few moments of peace and freedom, away from her mother's control.

She crossed the road, taking her time.

"Miss Farrin, please speed up. I must get you home."

"What's the big hurry? Nothing is happening at home."

"After I take you home I must go to your father's building site."

"Take me to the site with you," Farrin suggested. "I don't need to go home right away."

She got in the backseat and closed the door.

Ahmad hesitated then climbed behind the wheel. "Your mother told me to bring you right home."

"I'd like to see my father," Farrin said. "Come on, let's go. He won't mind, and it will be an adventure."

"Your mother will not want you to have an adventure."

"My father will," Farrin said. When Ahmad didn't start the car, she added, "And he's the one who hires and fires. Didn't you say you were in a hurry?"

Ahmad started the car.

They drove north, past the shops and the pizza place that Farrin longed to explore on her own. They passed the turnoff to Farrin's house and kept on going. The houses and apartment buildings soon gave way to scrubland, where Afghan refugees camped and the Alborz Mountains looked like they could fall right over and crush everything whenever they wanted to.

Looming ahead, still dwarfed by the mountains but bigger than everything else, was Evin Prison. High walls surrounded it. Farrin caught brief glimpses of the buildings that made up the prison compound as they traveled up hills, but lost sight of them again when they dipped into the valleys.

"My principal is an interrogator at the prison," Farrin said.

"I beg your pardon?"

"The principal at my school," Farrin said. "In her spare time, she goes to the prison and interrogates people. Probably tortures them too."

She could see Ahmad's face in the rearview mirror. His eyes were wide.

"What are you saying? She tortures people and she is allowed to be principal? Around children? How is this possible? Do your parents know?"

"It's a joke," Farrin said quickly. "She doesn't really do it. People say she does it because she's so mean to everybody. It's a joke. Don't you have jokes in Afghanistan?" she added meanly.

Ahmad's eyes went back to their normal size. "Prison is nothing to joke about," he said.

"Have you been to prison, Ahmad?"

"It's nothing to joke about," was all he would say.

He turned off the highway that led through the mountains to the Caspian Sea and onto a track road that was all dust and potholes.

"You'll have to wash the car again," Farrin said as the dust rose up around them like a fog.

There was war damage along the side of the road—bombed out military trucks so thickly covered in dust that they almost looked like giant boulders.

Farrin's mother was born to privilege; her father was an important general in the Shah's army, and they counted members of the royal family among their social acquaintances. As the revolution heated up, Farrin's grandfather read the signs and fled the country with her grandmother. But they left her mother behind. Farrin's mother had married someone they disapproved of, so they abandoned her to her fate.

Farrin's mother never let her father forget what she had given up for him.

Farrin's father had been a soldier on the military base where Farrin's mother lived with her parents. A member of one of Iran's nomadic tribes, as a child he had rolled into a campfire during his sleep. The burn fused the skin on the fingers of his right hand in such a way that he could not fire a gun, but this did not exempt him from military service. He was made a quartermaster in charge of distributing supplies. He found he had a knack for organization.

His wife's connections found him a good government job after he finished his military service, but the revolution put him out of work.

When Farrin was a little girl, her parents would argue over dinner. "You're a useless sand-lover," Farrin's mother would call him. "I'm surprised you know how to use a fork. Because of you, I had to sell all my gold." It was a common refrain. Both Farrin and her father learned to continue eating their meal and just let her mother rant.

A woman's gold was her treasure, her protection against the rough course of the future. She'd be given pieces throughout her life, and they'd form part of her dowry. It was wealth that was solid and tangible, and could be worn to show everyone what she was worth.

"North of the city the land was empty," Farrin's father used to say. He delighted in telling and retelling the story of the route they took to their new wealth. "This land was cheap. It was rocky. It was no good for crops and not at all pretty to look at. No one wanted it. No one but me, that is!"

Gold changed hands and the land became theirs. Farrin's father knew nothing about construction, but he studied everything he could find at the library. More gold went for building supplies. Although the Afghan refugees' labor was cheap, a number of them were educated and skilled. The first house went up, solid and beautiful. It sold for a good profit to a wealthy family eager to escape the overcrowding of the inner city. Farrin's father bought more land and more building supplies, and the family became entrenched in the building business.

"Are you sure your father will be okay with you being here?" Ahmad asked.

"Don't worry. He'll be happy to see me."

That much, Farrin was pretty sure she could count on. Her mother always looked a little pained when Farrin came into view. Her father generally smiled. She got out of the car.

They were standing in what was going to be a whole new neighborhood. Some of the homes were half finished, others were just cement blocks and rebar. The air was filled with the sound of hammers. A crane lifted supplies into the air.

Farrin spotted her father across the yard, deep in discussion with one of the workers. They were looking up at the shell of a building and didn't notice Farrin as she walked up to them.

"Hello, Father," she said.

He was surprised to see her, but still he smiled—all the while looking questioningly at Ahmad.

"I told him to bring me," Farrin said quickly. "I wanted to see you."

"Why come all the way out here?" her father asked. "You'll see me this evening."

Farrin searched her mind for an excuse. She looked around at the building supplies and all the activity—and then she had an idea. "I just thought it was time I learned more about what you do. Do you have time to show me around? Maybe I can go into the business when I get through with school."

Her father's smile grew into a grin. "You absolutely can! I don't have a lot of time today, but we can make a start. I am so happy that you are taking an interest in this!"

For the next twenty minutes, Farrin was stuck hearing about foundations and framing and how to save money on roofing tiles. At first she kicked herself for opening her mouth, but then she started to take an actual interest. At least it was something different.

"Maybe when you get older I'll bring you into the business

as a partner," he said. Then he winked. "No need to tell your mother about that part!"

Farrin agreed, although it was a stupid secret. There was no point to it, really. Her mother wouldn't care if she were interested in construction. Her family just liked to keep secrets.

Farrin noticed that the worksite had gone quiet. The hammers had stopped swinging and the saws were silent. Her father noticed the quiet at the same time.

All the men were looking at her.

"Why are they staring?" Farrin asked. "Is it because I'm a girl?"

"It's because you're a child," her father said. "They miss their families."

"Then it's good that I came."

"Not if it upsets them. I don't want them thinking about their children. I want them thinking about my buildings. Back to work!" he called out. "Let's go! These houses won't build themselves!"

Farrin left her father to his work and headed toward the car. She rounded the corner—and stopped in her tracks.

The trunk of her father's car was open. Ahmad was handing a box full of food to one of the Afghan workers.

Everyone froze.

Farrin took in the situation. She knew Ahmad earned no money, so the food probably came from the storeroom at home. And she doubted very much that her mother had given him permission to take it.

Another secret, she thought.

"Need any help?" she asked.

They didn't. The Afghans took the boxes of groceries and disappeared into the building site. Ahmad, ramrod straight again, opened the back door of the car. She climbed in and they drove away.

This was an interesting turn of events. Of course she'd keep Ahmad's secret. She'd even help him steal food from her parents' house. They had lots. Despite the food shortages caused by the war, her parents had enough money to buy anything they wanted on the black market.

But how could she use this information to her advantage? There must be something she could get out of the deal too.

"I'll keep your secret," she said.

Ahmad didn't respond.

She repeated herself as the car slowed down.

"There is some sort of gathering ahead," Ahmad told her. "It's blocking the street. I'm not sure I can turn around here."

Farrin leaned forward. All she could see were boys, lots of them.

"I'm going to see what's going on," she said.

"No! You must not do that! It's much too dangerous!"

Farrin had already opened the car door. "I'll be right back."

She pulled her scarf close around her face and checked that none of her hair was showing. After all, she was no fool. She walked toward the crowd, her heart beating hard. This was another new thing, being out in the world alone. Well, Ahmad was with her, but he was a servant. He didn't count.

It was turning out to be quite a day.

She knew without looking that Ahmad was behind her, keeping a close eye. Losing the boss's daughter would be a sure reason to get fired!

A small group of women, all in chadors, were standing off to the side. Farrin joined them and exchanged the traditional greetings. It was hard to hear over the boys' chants.

The street was full of boys. Most were around Farrin's age, a few older. Many were younger. They all wore red martyr's bands around their heads.

"We want to die for the revolution!" A cleric at the front was leading the chant through a loudspeaker hooked up to a car.

"We want to die for the revolution!" the boys cried.

"Death to our enemies!"

"Death to our enemies!"

"Death to Iraq!"

"Death to America!"

"We will be heroes in paradise!"

Farrin tried to tune it out. It was just another *basiji* rally, organized by the militia force to get the boys ready to go off to the front to fight the Iraqi army. She'd seen them before. The rally wasn't that exciting. Being out of the house without her parents was a much bigger thrill.

"They look younger with every rally," one of the women remarked.

"What are you saying?" another woman asked the first. "That sounds like criticism. Are you criticizing the government? Are you saying you would rather live under Saddam Hussein?"

"I'm saying that the pitch of the voices in paradise has risen very high in the last few years," the first woman said. "Two of my sons have taken their places in paradise. My youngest is in the middle of the rally today."

"Is that man following you?" A third woman interrupted the first woman to speak to Farrin. She pointed at Ahmad, who had left the car and was watching Farrin closely. "I think he is. He is following you! I will get the Revolutionary Guard to arrest him."

"No!" Farrin said. "He's with me. It's all right."

"What do you mean, he's with you? He's an Afghan. He's not your brother or your uncle or your father. Who is he?"

To be out in the world with a man who was not a relative could mean serious trouble for a girl. Farrin started to back away. Should she tell them Ahmad was a servant? Would that help or hurt?

Instead of answering, she hurried back to the car with Ahmad at her heels. In seconds, they were both inside.

"Get us out of here!" she said.

There was very little room to turn around. Ahmad drove up onto the sidewalk and swerved like he was in a car chase in a Hollywood movie. Farrin saw the women staring at them and then looking around for the Revolutionary Guard.

Farrin didn't need to tell Ahmad to drive fast. She checked the rear window as they sped away. No one was following them.

"Maybe one of these days I'll have a quick look around the shops after school," she said. "But perhaps you had better stay in the car when I do."

There was silence from the front seat as Ahmad considered his options.

Then he said, as Farrin knew he would, "Yes, Miss Farrin."

Pleased with herself, Farrin leaned back against the seat.

A pact had been made.

Four

The party was already underway.

Farrin could tell from the pile of shoes inside the front door that some of the guests had arrived. For now, all the shoes belonged to her mother's women friends. Their husbands would join them later. By the time Iraq started the evening's bombing, the house would be full of people celebrating the end of the world with a stiff drink and a bit of fun.

"Your mother wants to see you."

Ada relayed the message as soon as Farrin entered the house.

"How mad is she?"

Instead of answering, Ada asked, "How late are you?"

"I'll tell her it was my father's fault."

"That will work." Ada had been their housekeeper as long as Farrin could remember. She had witnessed even more family arguments than Farrin.

Farrin headed to the kitchen. From there, she would be able to look into the inner room, and gauge her mother's mood without being seen.

Farrin's house had a formal front room, where her father saw business colleagues and where the family's public image matched the spirit of the revolution. Stiff, formal furniture lined the walls underneath photos of the Ayatollah.

The front room led directly to the kitchen. Farrin pushed open the heavy soundproof door. Inside, the cook and other servants were scurrying around, preparing food for the party.

The kitchen had a pass-through window into the room behind it. Even though the window's shutter was closed, Farrin could hear the laughing voices and the clinking of tea glasses.

Later, she knew, the laughter would be supplemented with music, and the tea would be exchanged for something stronger.

Ever since Saddam Hussein had begun to bomb Tehran, Farrin's parents and their friends engaged in an almost-nightly movable party. It shifted from house to house, and as the bombing got rougher, the drinking got heavier.

Although she hated the people who attended the parties, Farrin preferred it when they came to her house, since her parents refused to let her stay home when they went to a party elsewhere. It was almost impossible to find a place to hide out at someone else's home. The adults were always sticking their nose into her business.

"What are you reading?" "What are you writing? School work? Why not see if we are still alive in the morning before you do your homework!" and "Why are you sitting all the way over here by yourself when the party is in the other room?"

When her parents hosted the celebration, it was easier to hide from all the guests. As long as no one saw her, no one thought of her. The trick was to get upstairs without being noticed.

Her evening would be ruined if she joined her mother and the other women. But if she didn't check in with her mother as directed, she'd be in trouble.

Farrin chose trouble over a ruined evening. She put some bread, fruit, cheese, and pastries on a plate, then left the kitchen the way she'd come in and headed up the stairs to her bedroom.

Farrin's house was the fifth they had lived in since the revolution. To save rent, her father often moved the family into the new homes he built. They would live there while the finishing touches were added. Since the family already had servants and security guards, her father never had to pay for new ones to take care of an empty house.

When her family moved into this one, the nicest one yet, Farrin's mother put her foot down and declared she was done with moving.

"My gold paid for all this," she declared. "This is where we will stay."

After she declared she liked it so much, she went about demanding changes, so many that the skilled laborers couldn't keep up with their other work. This house, like the others, had seen many fights. Farrin tried to stay out of it, since none of the fights brought her any advantage.

It was a relief to open the door of her bedroom, walk inside, then close the door behind her.

"A closed door," Farrin said out loud. "It's the best thing."

Especially at the end of a very long day.

Farrin's bedroom was not to her taste. Her mother had designed it to look like it came out of an American magazine called *Good Housekeeping*.

"You're too young to know what your taste is," her mother told her when Farrin objected to the fabric choices and paint colors her mother chose. The room looked almost exactly like the picture clipped from the magazine, with pinks and lemon yellows that might have suited a child half Farrin's age. The bookshelves held her mother's collection of international dolls, which Farrin never played with, as well as a wide variety of books in Persian and in English. The English books came from street vendors who sold private collections from pavement stalls. Most of the English bookstores in Tehran had been closed since the revolution.

Farrin recoiled a bit every time she walked into the room. It felt as if she were trespassing on the sanctuary of the child her mother had wished for. "But it has a door," she reminded herself. "A door that closes."

She hung her manteau on the hook, dropped her book bag on her bed, and put the plate of food down on her desk. Before flopping down in her easy chair, she took one of the videos off her bookshelf and popped it into the VCR, pressing Play and turning on the television set. The opening music of *The Night Stalker* was the perfect antidote to school and the stress of the day.

This was one of her favorite episodes, about a vampire let loose in Los Angeles. She focused on the grainy video and felt herself begin to relax.

Videos, music, magazines, and books were all hit and miss in revolutionary Tehran. Many things were forbidden, declared decadent and immodest but available to those with enough money. Farrin didn't know how it worked—who her father contacted or how he knew that person was on their side and would not report them to the Revolutionary Guard. All she knew was that, every so often, a man with a large briefcase would come to their house and leave them with forbidden items. And if she thought to tell her dad what she wanted—like books of ghost stories and scary movies—eventually the Briefcase Man would bring them.

She gave her eyes a rest from the fuzzy screen and turned to her bookshelves. Her gaze shifted from her collection of Edgar Allen Poe stories to *Dracula, Frankenstein,* and *Great American Ghost Stories.*

She hated that Principal Kobra had seen her demon story. How could a woman like that know anything about demons? Or about stories? Did she even have dreams? Principal Kobra was all hard edges and stern looks. Her imagination probably didn't extend beyond whatever torture she wanted to inflict on her students.

Farrin remembered the boys from the basiji rally. An idea came to her, something about Iranian demons on a battlefield. She grabbed her notebook from her book bag. How to write it? The idea was brilliant, she was sure about that, but it was just at the edge of her brain. In another second it would be sitting right where she could get at it and define it.

At that moment, of course, her mother burst into her room.

Farrin's mother was tall and striking, with the sort of ageless beauty and grace usually reserved for Hollywood stars and royal families. She was dressed in silks and beads, high heels and high hair. At least, Farrin assumed she was. She kept her eyes on her notebook and did not look up at the sound of the door slamming into the wall.

"You have the manners of a peasant."

"Hi, Mom," Farrin said. "How was your day?"

"Ada told you to see me as soon as you came home."

"Really? I didn't get that message."

"Ada says you did, and I'll believe her long before I believe you."

"That says a lot," said Farrin.

"Yes, it does. Why were you late? Look at me when I'm talking to you."

Farrin lifted her head and looked at her mother. "I was at the construction site with Dad. I wanted to learn more about the business."

"What for? You'll never work in it. I want you downstairs. Some of the ladies would like to hear you play."

"I'm busy," Farrin said. "I'm doing homework."

"Let me see."

Her mother made a move toward the notebook. Farrin held it to her chest.

"I thought so," her mother said. "Wasting time again. Downstairs, please. And try to put a smile on your face. It *is* a party."

"I think it is shameful to have a party when so many died in the bombing last night and even more will die tonight," Farrin said. "It's like 'The Masque of the Red Death' at your parties—everybody drinking and having fun and thinking they can just lock Death out of the castle, but Death comes in anyway."

"Oh, for goodness' sake, Farrin, must you be so dramatic about everything? So much has been taken from us. What is the point of living anymore if we can't have a little bit of fun now and then?"

"I don't think your parties are fun," Farrin said. "I think they are obscene when so many Iranians are suffering. I'm not coming down. Your ladies can meet the end of the world without my piano playing."

Her mother gave one of her exaggerated sighs, even though they had had no effect on Farrin for some time. "After all we've given her, you'd think a daughter would be grateful and try to please her mother by simply playing a happy little tune for some sad, frightened neighbors. But I understand. You exist at a much deeper level than all of us. You feel the pain of the universe, and I respect you for that."

In one smooth, decisive move, her mother crossed the room and swept up Farrin's food tray.

"You can feel the pain of others much more clearly if your stomach is not filled with decadent delicacies," her mother said before she left, slamming the door behind her.

Farrin threw her notebook at the door. Her mother was probably out of earshot already, not that it would have made any difference. The whole family slammed and threw things. It was like the background music for their daily lives.

"Tomorrow I'll get Ahmad to drive me to a grocery shop and I'll stock up on packaged food," Farrin said aloud. "Or, even better, I'll steal it from the pantry. And while I'm at it, I'll load up the car for Ahmad and his little band of Afghan workers."

Farrin's anger took the edge off her appetite for a few hours. She watched a few more episodes of *The Night Stalker*, wrote a bit on her demon story, and even did a splash of homework. As time passed, more people arrived and the party noises got louder.

Finally she was so hungry that she decided to chance it. She counted on her mother being too involved with her friends to even remember that she had a daughter.

She opened the door a crack. No one was in the hallway. Down the stairs, back through the formal sitting room and into the kitchen. The kitchen staff was washing dishes. Unlike Ada, these young women had no long history with her mother's family. Farrin doubted her mother even knew their names. Farrin did, though.

"Any food left, Zahra?" she asked one of the women.

"I'll make you up a plate," Zahra said.

"Don't be dainty," Farrin said. "Just dump the food on. I'm in a race against my mother. The first one to get back to my bedroom wins."

Zahra took a tray and started heaping on the bread, roasted chicken, feta cheese, and fruit. Farrin was just reaching into a bakery box for a couple of pieces of baklava when she felt a claw on her shoulder.

"Feeling the suffering of the Iranian people?" her mother asked.

"Oh, here is your lovely daughter!" One of her mother's friends stepped into the kitchen. "Farrin, your mother has been bragging about your piano playing. You will honor us with a small piece of music, won't you?"

"Of course she will," her mother answered for her. "She loves to play the piano for our guests."

With her mother's fingers like talons in her neck, Farrin headed for the inner room.

The first thing that greeted her when she opened the door was a large picture of the Shah of Iran. A cloud of cigarette smoke wafted around it, giving it a mysterious, mystic appearance. The next thing Farrin saw was the bar, a cabinet that held the family's liquor supply. The cabinet, which was usually locked, was now open, its contents littering tabletops all around the room. Rock and roll was coming from the stereo, and her parents' friends were dancing.

"Let's get this over with," Farrin said under her breath.

Her mother turned the stereo off and clinked a fork against her wine glass.

"Let me have your attention, please," her mother said. "I would like to introduce you to—well, you all know her already, so it is not an introduction, but I would like you to hear my daughter Farrin play the piano. Farrin, clear off that piano bench and sit down. And smile, for crying out loud!"

The bench had been a repository for empty glasses and full ashtrays. Farrin resisted the urge to sweep it all to the floor with her forearm. Instead, she carefully placed the detritus on the floor by the piano legs and sat down.

"Now I know she looks like a bit of a monkey, with that dark skin of hers," her mother said. "That's what I get for marrying into a family of desert-dwellers. But look beyond that ugliness, if you can, and just listen. All right, Farrin, don't just sit there. Start playing. And play well. Don't make me a liar in front of my friends."

Farrin looked to her father to see if he might say something in her defense, but he was too busy pouring himself another drink. He rarely stood up to her mother, anyway.

She wondered what to play.

For a moment, she considered playing something childish, and doing it badly, so that her mother would be humiliated. But then she thought about what the party was all about, and 'The Masque of the Red Death,' the Edgar Allen Poe story about people trying to keep the plague out of their party. And her fingers started to move across the keyboard.

The party stopped. There was no fidgeting, no clinking of glasses—all drinking and smoking ceased. *I'll show* them, Farrin thought at first as she pounded the keys defiantly, but soon she was drawn into the emotion of the music.

The words of Principal Kobra, the ones she had so cynically parroted back to her mother in order to appear morally superior, became words that had depth and meaning. People died last night. And more would die tonight as well, unless Saddam Hussein, the Ayatollah, and all their combined forces decided they were done fighting and were ready to go home and be still.

The bombs falling, the young boys rushing into the battlefield, the widows crying, the homes being smashed, the long, sad marches to the graveyards—all these things found their way into Farrin's playing. And the atmosphere of forced gaiety that had ruled the party and the lives of the adults fell away as the sorrow of the war entered the room.

The song came to an end. The ghosts of the notes still hovered over the piano, holding the peace over the gathering.

Farrin's mother shattered the silence.

She bent down low to talk right in Farrin's ear. "This is supposed to be a party," she snarled. "Are you so obtuse that you can't understand—?"

Saddam's bombs were louder than her mother's snarl.

The air raid sirens started going off after the first bomb exploded. The explosion was close enough to the house to knock some of the whiskey glasses off the tables, but not close enough to shatter the windows.

"Everyone—into the storeroom!"

Farrin's father shepherded the group, using his arms to direct everyone into the small room at the very center of the house. Built with a reinforced ceiling and lined with shelves, it acted as their bomb shelter.

The electricity went out. The house was so dark that people tripped over chairs and each other as they groped their way to the storeroom. Farrin was swept along in a clutch of people. She couldn't tell who they were.

Saddam and his army were in fine form that night, with plane after plane dropping bomb after bomb. Farrin counted four explosions before she got to the storeroom, where her father had at last discovered a flashlight with working batteries.

Farrin perched on a large plastic bin filled with bags of powdered milk. Someone lit a cigarette, immediately setting off a chain of others lighting up. Soon the little room was more smoke than air. Farrin coughed, but no one seemed to care.

"Put your cigarettes out, please," her father said. Farrin silently thanked him.

"How are we supposed to get through this without cigarettes?" That came from her mother. "Someone open the door a crack—that will bring in some fresh air. I don't suppose anyone thought to bring the Bordeaux."

Farrin hated her mother in that moment, then in the next, she wondered if her mother had the right attitude. What else were they supposed to do during a bombing? Cry? Pray? Sit and shake with fear? She had done all of those things before, but the bombs fell anyway. Maybe it was best to act as if everything were normal.

The bombing went on for a long time. Farrin's father and mother found their way to her in the dark and sat with their arms around her, as if simple bone and sinew could protect her from the military might of an army eager to destroy.

As the night went on the pretense of normality fell away. The house shook, and screams from the outside world seeped into the storeroom.

"Maybe we really will die tonight," someone said.

"Are you all right, Farrin?" her father whispered to her.

Farrin didn't answer. What was there to say? She just wanted the bombing to end. She wanted to be back in her bedroom watching *The Night Stalker* and grouching about her mother.

She closed her eyes against the darkness and tried to think of something—anything—that would take her head out of this tiny storeroom filled with drunk, smoking grown-ups and into a place where she had a life and a future. She tried to conjure up her demon story, and the prospects for fame and fortune as the story would be made into a big Hollywood movie.

None of that worked.

The thing that worked was something that she had not expected. She could not begin to explain it.

What brought her calm and a feeling of hope was a vision that rose from somewhere deep in her chest.

The vision was Sadira's face.

Part Two

Five

Farrin played it cool.

She saw Sadira at the flag raising in the school yard the next morning, but pretended as if she didn't. She kept looking over toward the other end of the line where Sadira stood, just in case… she didn't know what. In case Sadira disappeared? In case Sadira needed help remembering the words to the national anthem?

Stop staring, she told herself. But she couldn't make herself stop.

"Farrin, you had better come to the front," Pargol said. It was Pargol's turn to lead the school in morning exercises, and of course she saw Farrin not paying attention.

Sheepishly, Farrin tried to muster an expression of defiance but could only manage to look at the ground, at the sky, at the other students—anywhere but in Sadira's direction. What if Sadira was laughing at her? Even worse, what if Sadira had forgotten who she was?

Farrin was forced to stand right beside Pargol while Pargol gave the usual "Let's Work Hard For the Revolution and For Ayatollah Khomeini" speech that started every day. Pargol was particularly verbose when it came to revolutionary lingo. The thicker it was, the more she thought it made her look tough. Farrin thought it just made Pargol more boring.

"Where does she think it's going to get her?" Farrin whispered as Pargol droned on and on about fighting the Imperialists and the Iraqis. "She'll never get to run Iran. At best, she'll get to marry someone who runs Iran."

Farrin started to imagine Pargol as an older woman, still looking fierce and cross, standing behind a leader of Iran. The poor man would try to give a speech to the nation on television, and Pargol would poke him in the neck, correcting his grammar and telling him to sit up straight.

The image gave Farrin the giggles, and she had to make a big show of coughing to cover it up. As she raised her hand to her mouth, her eyes went to Sadira. Her face was sparkling with the same mischievous energy that Farrin felt.

She remembers me, Farrin thought.

The blood rushed up from her toes to the top of her head and did a wild dervish dance in the middle of her chest.

Finally, Pargol wound down. After her came Rabia, the school's Head Girl. Farrin paid attention to Rabia. This tall, calm girl held power by being smart and kind, and by setting the sort of example all the girls wanted to follow. Pargol held power simply because she was mean and not afraid to make others afraid.

Rabia briefly made an announcement about the mother-daughter tea coming up and asked for more volunteers to serve tea and clean up. Farrin knew her mother would not be going, so she saw no need to volunteer.

Principal Kobra stepped up to the flag post. She sent Pargol, Farrin, and Rabia back into line.

"This is the saddest duty I have to perform as your principal," she said. "I regret to inform you that another one of our students, Zohrey Bakshir, was lost in the bombing last night. She was in the junior school, in the second class. She was doing very well in arithmetic and loved to draw flowers. We will now have a moment of silence to think about her life and her family."

The school community went quiet.

Beyond the walls that surrounded the school yard, Farrin could hear the traffic of Tehran. She could hear peddlars and taxis and stray dogs barking. She heard a baby crying and a mother telling her small child to get up out of the dirt, she just washed those clothes! Outside the walls, life went on as normal. Inside the walls, the girls were mute.

This was not the first moment of silence at the school. It was not the second; it was not even the third. Farrin did not want to do the count.

There had also been moments of silence for family members—for Pargol's brothers and other girls' fathers, or uncles, or brothers.

Farrin though it was a wonder that there were any Iranians left at all.

Then one of the students behind her let out a loud belch. It was an accident, of course, but it was a good excuse to laugh. Farrin held it together, but around her she could hear some of the younger ones stifle giggles.

The assembly was brought to a close.

The day was, as usual, full of study and work. Farrin was in line for lunch when Sadira picked up a tray and stood in line beside her.

"Private joke?" Sadira asked.

"What?"

"This morning. During Pargol's speech. You were trying not to laugh. Was it a private joke or do you feel like sharing it?"

Farrin placed a plate of chickpea stew with rice on her tray and moved down the line toward the glasses of juice. "I was imaging Pargol married to a prime minister," she said. "He'd be giving a speech and she'd push him out of the way and correct everything he said."

"If any woman can be the leader of Iran, it will be Pargol, or someone with her temperament."

"It sounds like you like her."

"I don't have to like her to admire her," Sadira said, which Farrin had to admit was true. "Pargol is fearless. And she's bossy. She could make men listen to her. She could run the country one day. Iran has a history of powerful women."

"Pargol might end up running the country, but only because she'll have killed off all her enemies," Farrin said.

Sadira just laughed at that.

Farrin stood with her tray and surveyed the dining hall for a place to sit.

"Are you looking for your friends?" Sadira asked. "Do you usually eat with them?"

"I don't really have friends," Farrin said, then wished she could snatch back such a bold admission.

But Sadira admires boldness, she thought. So she added, "My mother doesn't like me to have a lot of friends. She thinks—well, she wants the family protected."

"Is your mother here today?" Sadira asked.

Farrin grinned. Her mother certainly was not there.

She spied an empty table. "How about over there by the window?"

They sat and ate lunch and watched the junior girls play in the school yard. Farrin knew the other students were looking at them. In all her time at that school, Farrin had never eaten lunch with anyone, except when there were no empty tables to sit at. And that wasn't really like eating with someone. It was more like a gang of cats tolerating a stray eating nearby, just for a little while.

At first, Farrin felt self-conscious. How should she hold her fork? Was there a bit of carrot stuck in her teeth? Could she drink her juice without spilling it all over herself and looking like a great big fool in front of her new friend? But then they started talking and Farrin forgot all about herself. She watched Sadira eat and laugh, and she wished the lunch hour would go on forever.

"Are those little girls crying?" Sadira asked, spotting a few of the juniors huddled together by the slide.

"Probably," said Farrin. "They're from Zohrey's class—you know, the girl who died."

"Let's see if we can help."

They carried their trays to the kitchen then went outside. For the rest of the lunch hour, Sadira talked with the juniors, hugged them, and comforted them. The juniors took to Sadira right away, but they eyed Farrin with suspicion. Clearly, they had heard that no one liked her. But by the time the bell signaled the end of lunch, they were including Farrin in their talk. She was even allowed to fix one of the girl's braids that had come loose.

"I'm glad we did that," Farrin said. "By making them feel better, it feels as if we've won our own little battle against Saddam Hussein."

Saddam got back at them during Farrin's algebra class. The air-raid sirens sounded through the area.

"Move, girls, quickly now. You know the drill." Pargol and the other monitors bossed everyone with calm efficiency. Soon the whole student body had gathered in the gym, the innermost room of the school. The teachers kept everyone in their class groups, and lessons resumed while planes flew overhead and explosions blew up parts of the nearby neighborhood.

It was a short raid. The all clear signal went off, but Principal Kobra announced that school was over for the day.

"Older ones, escort the younger ones home. If your families are not yet waiting for you outside, ask an older girl to walk you home. Those of you juniors from the south of the city, wait here and we will arrange taxis for you."

Farrin saw Sadira stand in line with the older girls who were volunteering to escort the younger ones home. She joined the line beside her.

"Let's walk together," she suggested. "It will be safer than if we walk alone after dropping off the juniors."

They escorted two sisters from the third and fourth classes, walked them to the front door of their home, and told the mother why they were early.

"I should not let them go to school," the woman said, sweeping the girls into her arms. "They should be here with me if Saddam hits us."

"Forgive me, ma'am, but you are wrong," Sadira said. "It is because of Saddam that your girls need to go to school. Men have run this world long enough, and they have made a mess of it."

The woman nodded. "Fighting is all they know. If they had ever been taught another way, they have forgotten it."

"So, we need educated women to take over," Sadira said. "I will personally look after your daughters if the sirens go off while we are at school. I will look out for them anyway, if that will make you feel better. If I can keep them from harm, you know I will do it. We must keep thinking of the future."

The little girls were thrilled. It was the practice of the senior girls to ignore the juniors at every opportunity, and to make sure the unworthy juniors knew they were being ignored. To have a senior girl watch out for them would give the young ones high status among their classmates. The girls begged their mother, and the woman relented.

"You just got yourself a job," Farrin said as they walked away. "I hope they won't be too much trouble."

Sadira laughed. "They're too much in awe of us to be any trouble."

Farrin liked the way she said "us," as if she took for for granted that she and Farrin would work together.

They were heading back to school, where Sadira could catch her bus and Farrin would wait for the car to arrive, when the sound of a pack of motorcycles made them stop.

"It's the Death Gang," Farrin said. "Let's see where they're going."

She turned and headed in the direction of the sound.

"The what?" Sadira asked.

"I call them the Death Gang, like American motorcycle gangs," Farrin explained. "Did you ever see the movie *The Wild Bunch*?" Sadira shook her head. Farrin was suddenly afraid she had said too much—*The Wild Bunch* wasn't exactly on the Ayatollah's permitted list. "Come on—it sounds like they are just around this corner."

She hurried ahead, hoping Sadira would follow her. Sadira did, and they rounded a corner, coming to a stop in front of a house where a missile had landed. Surrounding the home was a ring of motorcycles and Revolutionary Guards dressed in black.

The guards pushed people away from the rubble. "We have Saddam on the run!" they shouted. "We are raining death down upon him now. Today we destroy Saddam and Iraq. Tomorrow we destroy Israel and America and all the antirevolutionary forces that would bring back the Shah and imprison the Iranian people. Death to Saddam! Death to America! Death to Saddam! Death to America!"

The Revolutionary Guards kept shouting slogans as they encouraged the crowd to join in with them.

The crowd was silent.

Farrin had seen too many of these events. The Revolutionary Guard in black clothes and red headbands riding their motorcycles to bombed-out homes and whipping people up into a pro-war fervor. "Anger is more powerful than sorrow!" the guards would chant. "Shouting is more powerful than weeping! Fighting the enemy is more powerful than wishing on stars like little children do. Death to Saddam! Death to America!" The crowd would always join in the chants. They would always take up the shouts and the slogans—"Death to Saddam," who had bombed them and "Death to America," because America had supplied Saddam with the bombs.

This time, though, no one joined in.

The crowd of people around the bombed-out home just stood quietly, hands at their sides, shoulders slumped. Not one voice was raised. Not one sound came from anyone.

Farrin held her breath.

The Revolutionary Guards, armed and revved-up, pointed their rifles around at the crowd, and tried again.

"Death to Saddam! Death to America!"

No one made a sound.

A look of fear written on her face, Sadira gripped Farrin's arm and whispered, "Don't shoot them."

For a moment it looked like the guards would do just that before they finally lowered their guns.

The guards pumped their fists in the air a few more times and shouted for death before climbing back on their motorbikes and riding away.

The crowd did not cheer at their departure. Instead, they got back to work removing the rubble.

Sadira stepped forward to help. Farrin joined her.

"Everybody is out," an old woman said to them. "Three dead." She nodded at the bodies covered by blankets and placed off to the side. "Now we must try to get the house cleared enough that what's left of this family will have a place to sleep tonight."

Farrin and Sadira lifted rocks and stones and rubble, and stacked it in a tidy pile. Someone came with a truck and loaded the bodies onto the back.

Everyone worked without speaking. There did not seem to be anything to say.

Farrin worked alongside her new friend. She was exactly where she needed to be.

Six

It was a tinkling afternoon.

Teaspoons tinkled against china teacups.

Reflection off the silver tea service tinkled as the cups were refilled.

And the tinkling touch of Farrin's fingers on the ivory keys of the piano played a harmless, light classical tune.

It was all light, irrelevant, and forgettable.

On the first Monday of the month, her mother hosted the Bring Back the Shah Tea for Ladies of Culture. Held every single first Monday since Farrin could remember, it was a way for the lady fans of the Shah to learn about what her mother called "developments."

"There have been some *developments*," her mother would usually start, before going on to list the hopeful things that had happened in the preceding weeks.

Farrin was always pressed into service. Just after the

revolution, when she was small, her job was to wear a party dress and pass around a plate of almond cookies. The women would coo over her and pet her, then ignore her while they traded news about the Iranian royal family.

The Shah—Mohammad Reza Pahlavi—died in exile in 1980. When Farrin learned of his death years later, she was surprised. With his photo in such a prominent place in her family's inner room, he seemed as sure and solid as the walls and the mountains.

"He died soon after the revolution," her mother said. "I'm sure I told you. You just weren't paying attention."

"So how can we bring him back if he's dead?"

Farrin had visions of a zombie-Shah, arms outstretched, walking heavily around the palace grounds and screaming for human flesh to eat.

"We'll make his son the new Shah," her mother said. "The crown prince will be our salvation from the rabble that now rules over our land."

Farrin tinkled her way through the vacuous piece of music while the ladies drank their tea. She thought about that conversation with her mother, and wondered about using the zombie-Shah in her demon story. Or maybe the Shah could have been bitten by a wolf at his summer villa in the hills and comes back as a werewolf every full moon. Or—even better—the Shah could be a vampire, hiding in the darkness during the day then coming out at night to feast on the blood of his own people.

Farrin began to get excited. Vampires, werewolves and zombies weren't traditional Iranian demons, but who was to say such things could not exist here? Iran had ghouls and djinn of different sorts. Why not other monsters too?

In her excitement, she began pounding the piano keys instead of tinkling them, turning the piece of musical fluff she was playing into something like a military march.

All the ladies looked at her. Her mother frowned.

Farrin didn't apologize, but she did ease off on the pounding.

"I think it's time we begin," her mother said. Her mother was president of the club. It was a rotating honor, but even if someone else held the title, Farrin's mother held the power.

That was Farrin's signal to wind down the music.

Before the meeting could begin, there was a knock on the inner room door. Ada stepped into the room.

"Excuse me, ma'am. There is a telephone call."

"Take a message, Ada. I'm about to start the meeting."

"The call is for Miss Farrin," Ada said.

Farrin had never received a phone call before. Sometimes she was put on the phone to say hello to some relative or other, but no one had ever called just to talk to her.

"Who's calling *you*?" her mother asked in a tone that made it clear the caller was likely a criminal or an idiot.

"I don't know," Farrin admitted.

"It's someone from school," Ada said. "A Miss Sadira. She's calling about a homework assignment."

"Go," said her mother. "But don't be long. Our secretary has seen fit to come down with a headache. I'll need you to take minutes."

Not even the thought of playing secretary to her mother's silly friends could dampen Farrin's excitement. But she didn't rush to the hallway; she played it cool, as if a phone call from a friend was an everyday event. She didn't want her mother bothering her with a bunch of questions afterward.

"Hello?"

"Farrin? It's Sadira."

Farrin felt her stomach flip.

"Oh, hello," she said, continuing the cool act.

"Is this a bad time?" Sadira asked.

Maybe she'd played it too cool. "No, this is good. This is really good, actually. It got me out of one of my mother's meetings."

Farrin wanted to snatch her words back. These sorts of questions were the ones her mother was so afraid of.

"Well, she calls them meetings, but they're just these gatherings of all her women friends," Farrin continued. "Once a month they meet for tea and gossip. Mom likes me to be here to hand around refreshments."

"A gathering of women," Sadira said. "That sounds like fun. Maybe I could come over sometime and help serve."

Farrin would love to see her mother's reaction to Farrin bringing a stranger into their foolish little gatherings. She wondered if she would ever have the nerve to make it happen. With Sadira, even the worst situation would be all right.

"That would be great," Farrin said. "But my mother is—well, she's kind of peculiar."

"Parents are a challenge," Sadira agreed, "although I know

my mother would have liked you. I think you would have liked her, too."

"Farrin—you're needed!" Farrin's mother stuck her head into the hallway. "How long does it take to ask about a homework assignment?"

"I'll be right there," Farrin told her, then, in a formal voice she said into the phone, "We need to read the section on botany and then draw and label a plant native to Iran."

Her mother backed out the door and Farrin relaxed.

"You have to go?" asked Sadira.

"I probably should, or she'll keep interrupting us."

"Must be nice, having someone watch over you so closely."

"I guess," Farrin said. "Not always. Doesn't your father watch you?"

"My father is too sad," Sadira told her. "He's better now than he was, but he still isn't the way he used to be. He expects me to do the right thing. I like being trusted, but it would be nice, too, to have him ask who I was talking to at school or whether I've done my homework."

Farrin didn't know how to reply to that.

"So, I guess I'll see you in class tomorrow," said Sadira.

"I'll be there," Farrin said. Then she remembered. "Did you have a question about a homework assignment?"

Sadira's laugh made Farrin feel as if they were in the same room.

"I just felt like calling you," Sadira said. Then she hung up.

Farrin floated back to the inner room and her mother's meeting.

She sat down and took up the writing pad and pen.

"...We received this lovely letter from a woman in Toronto who says we should keep striving for a return to the monarchy," her mother was saying. "I think, judging from her many references to Queen Elizabeth, that she is under the impression that we want the British monarchy to rule Iran, but I dare say that Queen Elizabeth would certainly be a more civilized ruler for us than that bearded *Ayatollah*. Let me read to you what she says—"

The meeting droned on and on.

Farrin dutifully made notes. She was trying harder these days to be more cooperative with her mother. Less defiance meant smoother days, as it allowed her to fade into the background of her mother's world.

When the meeting finally broke up, her mother asked for Farrin's notes to add to the binder of minutes. Farrin took a quick look at the paper and crumpled it up.

"My pen broke," she said, balling the paper up as tight as it would go. "There is ink blotched all over it. I was paying attention, though," she said, as she quickly backed away and headed toward her room. "I'll write you out a nice, clean copy!"

A lecture about carelessness followed her all the way upstairs. Farrin closed the door to shut out the sound of her mother's voice before sitting on the middle of her bed.

With trembling hands she flattened out the paper.

There, in letters big and small, in Persian letters and in English, in pictographs dripping from the point of a moon, Farrin had written, over and over—

Sadira.

Seven

"'The morning stars sing together, and all the sons of God sing for joy.'"

Farrin looked from Sadira to her father Haj Nadir, to Ahmad, and to Rabbi Sayyed, the other guest in the front room of Sadira's house.

Sadira's father spoke in a calm, quiet, almost soothing voice. An older man with smiling eyes and a long beard, he was dressed in traditional robes and a cleric's turban. He gazed up at a point beyond the wall while he quoted, almost as if he were talking to the spirits. When he was finished, he lowered his head and smiled slightly as he looked around the room. His eyes landed on Farrin.

Farrin could tell that some kind of response was required, but she had no idea what to say.

She was visiting Sadira with her mother's permission, after much persuasion by her father.

"A friend is a great thing to have," Farrin's father said. "If our daughter has the gift of a friend, who are we to stand in her way?"

"We don't know anything about this strange girl or her family," her mother said. "This is an outsider who could be part of the Revolutionary Guard's spy network. She could bring down our whole operation here."

As far as Farrin could tell, the "whole operation" consisted of ladies raising their tea cups to old photos of the Shah, but she kept quiet and let her father do the arguing.

"Sadira doesn't have to come here," her father said. "Farrin may visit her at her house."

Farrin didn't know how she would explain it to Sadira when the time came to return the visit, but she left that problem for another day.

Ahmad was instructed to drive both girls to Sadira's house after Friday's half-day classes, and to bring Farrin home when the evening meal was done. "And I want a full report of everything," her mother had told him.

By this time, Farrin had helped Ahmad smuggle several trunk-loads of food to the Afghan workers. She was pretty sure he would give her mother nothing to disapprove of about the visit.

Sadira's father had welcomed them warmly, ushering them inside to sit in the most comfortable seats.

"I will wait for you in the car," Ahmad told Farrin, but Haj Nadir wouldn't hear of it.

"Come, Brother, we are all the same in the eyes of God.

You will enter my home and be my guest for however long we are honored to have you with us."

Farrin had helped Sadira prepare tea and dishes of candied almonds, and now they were all sitting together in the small front room on narrow mats that lined the walls. It was a very plain room. The only decorations were two photographs: one of Ayatollah Khomeini and the other of Mecca. Farrin found the room surprisingly easy on the eyes, with no clutter or shock of contrasting colors.

She struggled to figure out what she was feeling. Free, she decided. She was feeling free. Her mind could rest in a room like this.

Maybe I should redo my bedroom, she thought. All cushions. Simple and comfortable.

Well into the afternoon, they drank tea while Haj Nadir asked the girls about their studies. The men shared some light incidents from their school days and Farrin found that she was enjoying herself.

Then Haj Nadir said this strange thing about the morning stars singing. Clearly he wanted Farrin to respond, but she had no idea what was expected. And she did not want to look foolish in front of Sadira.

"It's from the book of Job," Rabbi Sayyed said. "Chapter thirty-eight, verse seven. 'Tears may come at nightfall, but joy comes in the morning.'"

"The book of Psalms," said Sadira. "I don't know which one, but I believe you have made an error, Rabbi. I believe the correct version is, 'Tears may linger at nightfall.'"

"She is correct, Rabbi," said Haj Nadir. "The word is 'linger.'"

"I concede to the correction," the rabbi said with a smile and a slight bow of the head.

Now it was Sadira's turn.

"'Those whose sins have perished, whose doubts are destroyed, who are self restrained and are intent on the welfare of all other beings, these obtain God's everlasting joy.'"

That one stumped both Haj Nadir and the Rabbi. Ahmad had the answer.

"That is from the Bhagavad Gita," he said. "For a few years I was a refugee in India, before being a refugee in Pakistan and now a refugee in Iran. I studied the Hindu holy book, in my small way, of course."

"That is the only way to study holy books," the rabbi said. "We can spend a lifetime in study and still understand very little by the end of our days."

Then what's the point? Farrin wanted to ask, but didn't.

"We do this study to bring us closer to the infinite goodness of God," Haj Nadir said, almost as if Farrin had spoken. "Ahmad, do you have a quote you would like to share with us?"

Ahmad thought for a moment before he said, "'Much silence and a good disposition, there are no two works better than these.'"

"That's from the Hadith," Farrin announced, surprised that she knew. Something from her religion classes at school had obviously stuck with her.

Then it was her turn to come up with a quote and she

mentally kicked herself for opening her mouth. The only quotes that came into her head were from *The Night Stalker* and Elvis Presley, and she didn't think "You Ain't Nothin' But A Hound Dog" would fit the mood of the afternoon.

Finally, she had one. It was the verse from Proverbs that Principal Kobra was fond of quoting in front of her students.

"'Even a fool, if he holds his peace, is thought wise; keep your mouth shut and show your good sense.'"

For a moment, the little room was quiet, and Farrin was suddenly afraid she had offended everyone. But then they laughed, and the rabbi guessed correctly that the quote came from the book of Proverbs.

"Rabbi Sayyed and I have been playing this game since we were boys," Haj Nadir said. "We played it with our fathers, who played it when they were boys with their fathers, who played it when they were boys with their fathers."

"I hope this tradition can continue between our two families," Rabbi Sayyed said. "Your good sons have passed on. My children have gone to Israel. But your daughter is becoming a learned woman and a blessing upon you. She will find a way for the game to continue."

"Perhaps Farrin will take up the game, and it can continue, passed now from mother to daughter for generations to come."

Farrin helped gather up the tea things and take them out to the little kitchen, leaving the adults to talk. "Father is so much better today than he has been in a long time," Sadira said. "I think it is because he likes you, and it does him good to see me happy."

Sadira's house was in the southern part of Tehran, a small section in a huge sprawl of tiny homes and apartment buildings. Ahmad had parked the car several blocks away. The streets around Sadira's house were wide enough only for people, bicycles, and motorbikes.

They washed up and chopped vegetables for the evening meal. The stove, like the house, was small—just two gas burners and no oven. There was no fridge, and the room's only light came in through a small window.

"You don't have a light in here?"

"The only electricity we use is in my room, so that I can have a proper light to study."

"You don't use electricity in the rest of the house?" Farrin had never heard of such a thing. "How do you have light at night?" She guessed there was no television set, either.

"We have kerosene lamps," Sadira said. "Up until this year, at night I would go out to the streetlight in the next block and study. There are several serious students in this block—girl students—and we would sit together. But then some neighborhood boys decided that they deserved our spot more than we did. So my father consented to an electric light in my room."

"You studied under a streetlight?"

"In this area, it is not unusual. But the light is not good for reading. I would get headaches."

As Sadira prepared everything for supper, Farrin tried to copy her, but her own hands were clumsy and held the knife awkwardly. Farrin's family had always had servants in the kitchen, so she never learned how to do even the simplest of things. It was fun, helping Sadira.

They finished their work, then Sadira took Farrin to see her room, the only other room in the house.

"My father sleeps and studies in the front room where we were," Sadira said. "This is where I study and sleep."

Sadira's room looked much like the front room but with a bit more color. The floor cushions were encased in a delicate green-blue material that reminded Farrin of the color of a clear sky at sunrise. A small cupboard held Sadira's belongings.

"Can I show you something? It's sort of a secret. Although you already sort of know about it from the first day I met you."

"Of course, you can tell me. I won't say a word."

Sadira opened her cupboard door. Inside, the tidy shelves held folded clothes and well-arranged books. It made Farrin want to tidy her own room.

Sadira lifted a santour out of the cupboard and put it on the floor. She opened the drawstring on a cloth bag and took out the little hammers used to strike the strings.

"It was my mother's" Sadira said. "She was an expert player. She taught me. When I play it now, it's like she's beside me. We lost almost everything when our house was bombed, but the santour was hardly damaged. Just here," she added, showing Farrin the corner that had some dents and scuff marks. "I know it's not exactly allowed by the government, but my father thinks that rule will change. He likes it when I play, as long as I do it quietly, because it reminds him of happier days.

"Will you play something for me?"

"In a moment. I have to tell you that there's more to my secret. Not even my father knows. I take Iranian classical music and I blend it with modern music, like rock and roll from the Turkish stations on the radio. Do you know the Rolling Stones?"

The Rolling Stones was one of the bands her parents played at their parties. Farrin knew them quite well.

"This is my version of 'You Can't Always Get What You Want,'" Sadira said. She began to play quietly. The combination of the beautiful Iranian notes and trills with the hard rock beat of the song was something Farrin had never heard before.

"It's wonderful!" said Farrin. "You should do that on the radio. People would love it."

"People might love it, but the government would hate it. Maybe someday. My father says things are always changing, that we learn from history that nothing ever stays the same for very long."

"Now I'll tell *you* a secret," Farrin said. "I'm writing a book. I'm planning on making it into a movie or a television show when it's done. Maybe you could write the music for it."

"What sort of book?"

"It's about an Iranian girl who fights demons. Iranian demons, mostly—like ghouls and djinn—but also other demons, like vampires and things."

"Why?"

"Why what?" Farrin asked, a little disappointed that Sadira didn't seem to get it. "Why would I write the book?"

"No, why does the girl fight the demons?" Sadira asked. "Does she want their power so that she can do evil things herself, or does she want to make the world a kinder place?"

Farrin thought for a moment. She had never considered that question. She liked the idea of having lots of power, since she never felt as though she had any, but, then...what would she do with the power once she had it? Making the world better might be fun, she decided.

"She's fighting to improve things," Farrin said. "She's more like Rabia, the Head Girl, than Pargol."

"Could I do it with you?" Sadira asked.

"You want to write the story with me?"

"No, I don't think I have enough imagination. But I would like to fight demons with you. Could you put me in the book? Could the story be about two girls who fight demons?"

Farrin's mind was in a whirl. "We'll make a club," she said, getting excited. This is what friends did in stories. They made clubs, like her mother and her tea-drinking, Shah-loving friends. Only Farrin and Sadira's club would be fun and useful, not silly and pointless.

"A demon-hunting club," Sadira agreed. "But no silly rules or officers. We'll just look for demons wherever we go and deal with them on the spot."

"And not tell anyone," added Farrin. "We'll be protecting the world and no one else will know about it. They'll go on about their ordinary lives, completely unaware that they have just been saved from a horrible, eternal death by two beautiful young girls who are still in high school."

"And you will write down all our adventures in your book, but like a story, so that no one will know they are true. You could be like Dr. Watson writing about Sherlock Holmes."

Farrin was shocked. "You know about Sherlock Holmes? Your father allows you to read those books?"

Sadira laughed. "My father is a cleric and a very holy man, so some people believe he thinks only about God. Well, of course he *does* do a lot of thinking about God. My mother once told me that he used to be stern and narrow-minded."

"What changed him?"

"He was sent to prison by the Shah. He was held there all alone for a very long time. The secret police force would only take him out of his cell to torture him. He had to rely on his mind and his faith to see him through. That's when he came to the conclusion that God gave us brains to be able to learn and think for ourselves. But he generally doesn't notice what I read. When he was going through that sad time, I read anything I could find, just so I wouldn't feel so lonely."

"You won't be lonely ever again," Farrin said. "It's a pact, then—we're the Demon-hunting Girls of Iran!"

Sadira grabbed hold of Farrin's hands, squeezed them tightly, and then released them.

It was over in a moment, but Farrin felt that her hands were now magical, full of electricity and special powers.

They left Sadira's room to finish preparing the evening meal. Farrin enjoyed cooking with her friend, and vowed to herself to learn more from their cook at home, so that Sadira would be impressed.

As they worked and talked, Farrin overheard bits of the men's conversation in the front room. The men were discussing the war in Afghanistan and the war with Iraq. She heard Ahmad's voice contributing to the discussion, and she was glad he was not outside, sitting alone in the car.

The rabbi left before the meal was ready. He had to go home to his own Sabbath dinner.

After supper, Farrin and Sadira went with the others to the mosque and sat with the other women during the service. Ahmad was with the men.

After the service, the girls waited outside for the men to finish talking and come to find them.

"Look at that moon," Sadira said. "I don't think I've ever seen a moon so bright."

"It's shining right down on us like a spotlight," Farrin said.

It was strange. She knew that the square outside the mosque was crowded with worshippers and the streets were full of noisy cars, but it felt like she and Sadira were all alone in Tehran.

"It's shining down on the two of us," Sadira said." She looked at her watch. "It's almost nine o'clock," she added. "Let's make another pact. Let's look at the moon every night at nine, and that way, if we are not physically together, we will be together in spirit."

"The nine o'clock moon," Farrin agreed, holding still but wanting to swirl and dance all over the square. "Every night," she promised.

Then the men appeared and broke the spell.

"You look like you've had a good day," Ahmad said as he drove her home.

Farrin watched Tehran go past her window.

"The best," she said. "I had the best day."

She was answering Ahmad, but she was talking to Sadira.

From her window she could see the moon, bright and full, shining down on Iran. *Sadira can see the same moon*, she thought. She checked her watch. It was just nine o'clock.

The nine o'clock moon, she thought.

Every night. Every night.

Eight

The whole school was assembled in the gymnasium.

They all stood. It was the only way that everyone could fit.

An assembly of this sort would usually take place outside, but in the school yard it would not have been possible for the students to see the small television screen.

Even in the gym with the lights dimmed, the screen was difficult to see. Farrin stood with her class in straight rows toward the back, sternly guarded by Pargol. Sadira was three rows behind her.

The gym was hot. The school community had been assembled for a while, waiting for the Ayatollah Khomeini to speak. They waited in silence while the newscasters droned on and on, filling in airtime until the leader was ready.

The juniors were starting to get restless when the Ayatollah finally appeared.

"It is with a heart of bitterness that I announce an end to

the war with Iraq," he said. "I would like to repeat this. The war with Iraq is now at an end."

There was silence in the gym. Principal Kobra turned the volume up on the television. This increased the sound of static as much as it increased the sound of Khomeini's words.

"Over one million of our Iranian brothers and sisters have died in this conflict. Millions more have been wounded, and millions have had to flee their homes," the Ayatollah added. "It was not a war we started. It was not a war we wanted. It was a war started by Saddam Hussein and backed by the United States of America. One million Iranians dead! So the end to this terrible war is not a time for celebration but for mourning."

The camera then zoomed in on the Iranian president's face. "We will abide by the cease-fire completely."

The Speaker of the Iranian Parliament added, "There should be no violations on the front, and God forbid not one unauthorized bullet should be shot."

Then Ayatollah Khomeini reappeared.

"The end of the war does not mean the Iranian revolution is without enemies. We know that there are forces inside our country that colluded with Saddam Hussein, that collude still with the Americans. They are betrayers of the revolution and all that Iran stands for. I would like now to speak directly to those enemies. If you thought you were safe because we were busy fighting for our lives against the imperialist lackeys who would bring crashing down everything we have built, know this—the revolution is stronger now, Iran is stronger now, and the Iranian people are stronger now than ever before. We will hunt down these enemies of the state, and we will deal with them in a way that will leave no doubt in the minds of everyone who is in control of Iran."

Farrin got a cold feeling as the speech went on. She tried to talk herself out of it. Surely Ayatollah Khomeini was talking about people who were plotting against him and the other leaders of the revolution—*really* plotting, not pouring tea for bored, privileged ladies like her mother did.

But what if people like her mother were the sort of enemies the Ayatollah meant? Farrin didn't think she could classify her mother as a good person; she did some charity work, but only when others were looking and only as little as she could get away with. But did that make her a bad person? Or just a frivolous one? And while it was not exactly good to be frivolous, surely it was not a crime, either. If the Ayatollah went around gathering up all the frivolous people in Iran, surely the country would be more in prison than out of it. *Not that Iran has many frivolous people*, she thought quickly, in case someone was able to read her thoughts and say she was being critical. She only meant that her mother might like the Shah more than the Ayatollah, but was that really a danger to the nation? Around and around the thoughts went in Farrin's head.

When the Ayatollah stopped speaking and the screen went dark, Principal Kobra picked up where he left off, telling the students to be vigilant and to report to the authorities any suspicious activity. At that, Farrin had heard enough. The chill she felt changed to a stifling heat, and she fell to the floor in a dead faint.

From far away she could hear the students gasp and Pargol sneer at her to quit being so dramatic. Then she felt a cool cloth bathe her wrists and neck. She opened her eyes. Sadira was bending over her, and behind her a ring of faces laughed down at her.

Pargol's face was in the ring. But she wasn't laughing.

"How many brothers did you sacrifice for the war?" Pargol asked. "Is your father still alive? Was your house bombed? No. Nothing happened to you. So get up. Shame on you for drawing such unseemly attention to yourself."

Sadira helped Farrin stand.

"Are you all right?" Sadira asked.

Farrin nodded.

"Something is wrong," Sadira said. "What is it?"

"Not here," Farrin managed to whisper.

They filed back to class, where their teacher dismissed them early. "Many of you will have graves to visit," the teacher said. "This is not time off to laugh and play in the streets. Remember what our Ayatollah said. This is a time of mourning. I trust that you will all conduct yourselves accordingly."

She glared right at Farrin. It was so unjust.

Farrin took time to fill her book bag, hoping to find the chance to talk with Sadira without Pargol listening in. But Pargol did not cooperate. She sneered at both girls. Then, with a jerk of her head, Pargol motioned for Sadira to leave the classroom.

Sadira glanced first at Farrin, who nodded that it was okay for Sadira to go ahead.

"Looks like you finally found someone to be your friend," Pargol said as Sadira headed out. "I hope she's prepared to pay the price."

"The price for friendship?" Sadira asked. "A good friend is beyond price."

Pargol made a mocking face. Sadira flashed Farrin a smile, and with a wave, she started to leave the room.

Pargol blocked the door to Farrin. "That was some little stunt you pulled in the gymnasium," Pargol said.

"That was no stunt," Farrin said, trying not to be intimidated. "I just fainted. It was the heat."

She should have stopped there, but Farrin couldn't resist adding, "You've heard of fainting? It's something humans do."

Pargol stepped closer, so that she was breathing right on Farrin.

"You forget that you are no one," she said. "You think you are someone, with your new friend and your dumb little story about demons. You think your illusions will protect you? Nothing will protect you. I can crush you any time I feel like it."

"You seem shorter," Farrin said. "Did I grow a little, or did you shrink?"

Pargol just smiled at Farrin's insolence. "A bug can still make a loud noise up until the moment it is stepped on," she said. "Don't even try to save yourself. Your days are numbered."

"*Que sera, sera*," Farrin said, quoting one of her mother's Doris Day records. She pushed past Pargol and went off to find Sadira.

Sadira was in the school yard. "What was that all about?" she asked.

"Pargol always thinks she has some big secret," Farrin said. "It gives her a feeling of power."

"I mean, in the gym. What happened?"

Farrin wanted to tell her, but was not sure how it would be received. "Can we walk for a bit?" she asked. "I'd like to get away from the school."

They had not expected early dismissal. Ahmad was not waiting for Farrin, and Sadira's father was not expecting her home. They had time to walk.

The streets were beginning to fill up with people who had heard the Ayatollah's announcement. His prediction was right—there was no jubilation, no rejoicing. Farrin had the impression that the whole mood of the country was confusion. What had it all been for?

She asked Sadira about it.

"If we hadn't fought back, Saddam would have taken over Iran," Sadira said. "We had to fight."

"I guess so," Farrin said. "We didn't gain anything, though."

"My father says that if anything is gained by war, it should be given back, because something gained through violence is a form of theft."

The girls walked up the street to a little park at the top of a hill. They sat down on a bench; from there, they could look down in all directions. Farrin reached for a balled-up scrap of paper that was rolling about in the breeze. It was a piece of one of the illegal women's rights flyers that popped up every now and then. Farrin smoothed it out, then folded it up and put it in her pocket as she tried to gather her courage.

"I have something to tell you," Farrin said, "and I'm afraid to, because I think it will make you not want to be my friend anymore."

"I can't imagine anything that would make me want that," Sadira said.

"It's about my parents," Farrin said. "Mostly, it's about my mother."

She paused.

"Go on," Sadira said. "It's okay."

"Remember," said Farrin. "It's my mother, not me. The Shah put your father in prison. My mother loves the Shah. Even though he's dead, she still loves him, and she loves the monarchy."

"That's it? That's your big secret?"

"She has a group of ladies who also love the Shah. They're trying to bring back the royal family."

"That sounds dangerous," Sadira said. "How are they doing this?"

"I'll tell you everything, if you want to know."

Sadira was silent a while. Farrin could see that she understood that by agreeing to hear, she was also agreeing to keep Farrin's secret.

"Before you tell me anything," Sadira began, "could you tell me first if they are doing anything against the law?"

Farrin wasn't sure if it was against the law to hang the Shah's picture in their house. She knew it wasn't a good idea, but was it actually illegal? She didn't know. Her parents had alcohol in the house, though, and that was illegal. So were the videos brought by the Briefcase Man.

"They are breaking the law," Farrin said, "but not in big ways. They drink wine and whiskey, and watch illegal videos. I have illegal videos in my room, but I don't drink alcohol. Those are the only illegal things they do, I'm sure. They're not doing anything to bring down the revolution. They're too silly for that."

"All right, then tell me," Sadira said.

"My mother invites ladies to tea," Farrin said, "and they talk about bringing back the royal family. But I don't think they actually do anything else. Just talk."

"And what do you do when they are drinking tea?"

Farrin was embarrassed, but she could not stop confessing now. "I play piano and pass around the cookies."

"That's what you were doing when I phoned you?"

Farrin nodded.

"What do you think of the Shah?" Sadira asked.

Farrin shrugged. "Why do I have to think anything? All my life, at home it's been 'the Shah is wonderful,' and at school it's been 'the revolution is wonderful.' I would just like to be left alone to grow up and figure things out on my own."

"Well, let's do that, then," Sadira said. "Our parents have minds of their own. We're not responsible for them. My father loves lima beans. Just because I am his daughter, does that mean that I must also love lima beans?"

The question seemed so wonderfully silly in the middle

of such a serious conversation that Farrin just had to laugh. Sadira laughed with her.

They were still laughing when the first of a group of young boys came marching past.

They were basiji boys, back from the war. For days now, others had been seen marching back from the front. Many of the boys were in bandages. Some limped. Others stared, their eyes looking wild and crazed.

They came first in a trickle, heading down the street, stopping traffic, and making drivers honk their horns. They seemed to be attempting to march in formation, but their rhythm was off and they could not hold it. Too many of them were wounded, and they moved awkwardly, with weary gaits.

One boy, who looked younger than Farrin, had a bloody patch over one eye. He stopped before a wall where a large portrait of the Ayatollah had been painted.

Farrin nudged Sadira to watch.

For a long moment, the boy stood before the portrait, just looking up at it with his one remaining eye.

He's going to salute, Farrin thought.

Instead, the boy bent down to a mud puddle and scooped up a fistful of mud. His arm went back—and then he threw. The muck landed right on the Ayatollah's face.

He bent down again to get another fistful.

Farrin saw the black uniforms of the Revolutionary Guard heading up the hill. "They'll arrest him," she said. She and Sadira ran to the boy and pulled him away from the mud.

They kept his face down and hidden between them until the soldiers had passed.

"Are you all right?" Sadira asked the boy. "You are tired. Let us help you."

The boy just gave an anguished cry and wrenched himself away. He joined the line of basiji boys and shuffled away.

For a moment, Farrin and Sadira stared at the backs of the boys as they headed down the hill.

"The world is run by demons," Sadira said.

"We can't waste time," said Farrin. "My mother and her friends—they put off living until an event that may never happen. I can't do that. I can't put off my life."

Sadira agreed. "We can't postpone living. We never know when we are going to die. There could be another war at any time. We have to just live while we can. For me, that means doing everything the best that I can—cooking the best meals for my father, doing my best on all the exams, having the most possible fun I can have with you, my best friend."

"So, we will live, then," said Farrin. "We will live and work as though we could die tomorrow. And then we will have no regrets."

At that point, they turned to look in the direction the basiji boys had come from. Sadira let out a gasp.

As far as they could see, a line of boys in red martyr's headbands walked, limped, staggered, and crawled up the crest of the hill toward them. Many of them were weeping openly.

Sadira slipped her hand into Farrin's. They stood together like that for a long time, watching the boys.

"No regrets," said Sadira.

"No regrets," Farrin echoed, and she squeezed her friend's hand, their fingers so entwined that it was hard to tell where one hand ended and the other one began.

Nine

The school buzzed.

Farrin felt it as soon as she walked through the door. The air seemed alive with energy. Girls stood in their groups, gossiping as usual, but their posture was different. As Farrin walked past them, instead of closing ranks to exclude her, they turned to her.

She couldn't read their faces.

At first she thought they were laughing at her. That was the reason she usually drew students' attention, when they were looking for someone to ridicule.

Then she wondered if there had been another tragedy—something unexpected, since the war had been over for a while. She wondered who had died, and how.

But then one of the older girls left the group she was with and came over to shake Farrin's hand.

"Congratulations," the girl said.

"For what?"

"You don't know?" The girl turned to her friends. "She doesn't know. Let's show her."

The group swept her up. They put their hands around her waist and arms, and headed down the hall toward the main entrance.

Farrin usually entered the building through the side entrance—the one closest to the spot where Ahmad dropped her off. The main entrance was in the center of the building, where Principal Kobra's office and the main bulletin board were situated.

The bulletin board held announcements about after-school groups, detentions, monitor meetings, uniform sales, and other school business.

It was also the place where the half-term academic standings were posted.

As soon as the group started heading in that direction, Farrin knew—she *knew*—that she was about to have one of the most victorious moments of her life.

But was Sadira going to be up there with her?

She needn't have worried.

"You have done what nobody else has managed to do," one of the girls said. "You have beaten Pargol."

There it was, right up on the bulletin board, for everyone to see. Farrin's name was in second place, with a ninety-one percent average. Sadira's name was first, with ninety-three. Pargol's name appeared next, a distant third place, with eighty-eight percent.

"Here comes our first-placer! Three cheers for Sadira!"

The cheers rang out as Sadira stepped into the building and walked over to the bulletin board. Admiring girls immediately surrounded her.

Farrin grinned at Sadira, then stared again at the standings sheet. She could not take her eyes off that ninety-one percent by her name.

She had never been awarded a grade that high before. And it was her average grade for the term! That meant she had even higher grades in some of her individual classes. She was used to mediocrity, to doing just enough work to avoid attracting the teachers' attention. She had never made an effort.

Ever since she had begun to study with Sadira, Farrin's brain had worked more than ever before. The biggest thing she'd learned that term was self-discipline. It hadn't even been that hard, not once she learned how to clear her mind of distractions and focus in on the work. She and Sadira had studied during lunch hour away from the other girls, sitting on the floor of the gym with their books in front of them. Farrin had really paid attention in class, and in the evening, studying had given her the perfect excuse to use the phone to call Sadira with questions. She'd even studied in bed with her books propped up on her knees. Her videos of *The Night Stalker* had sat forgotten, gathering dust.

Farrin felt a slight twinge of worry. What would her mother say about her being in the second position? But she couldn't see how her good grades in organic chemistry could thwart her mother's efforts to bring back the Shah, so she decided not to tell.

"Our work paid off," Sadira said.

"I didn't know I had it in me," said Farrin.

Sadira grinned. "Oh, I knew you did. Just don't get any fancy ideas about pulling ahead of me!"

"Is that right?" Farrin laughed. "Next month my name will be on top!"

It was all part of their plan to feel alive as long as they could. Since work was part of life, if they had to work, they would *really* work. When they were in gym class, playing sports, they played hard. Whatever they did, they tried to do it full out.

The chattering suddenly died away as Pargol entered the hall and walked over to the bulletin board. But before the monitor could take a look, Sadira held out her hand.

"Congratulations, Pargol," she said. "Top three."

"What are you talking about?" Then Pargol saw the sheet. Her face turned to stone.

"I didn't know you were a scholar," she said to Sadira.

"My father spends a lot of time with books," Sadira told her. "He taught me how to study."

"Oh," said Pargol. "That explains it. You come by it naturally."

"Plus I work hard," Sadira said.

Pargol waved her off.

"You," she said to Farrin, "must have cheated."

The students all gasped at once. To accuse someone of cheating was serious. Cheating could mean getting kicked out of the academy. A cheater would disgrace herself and her family to such an extent that it was unlikely she would ever attend another school. Her family would marry her off as quickly and as quietly as possible.

Farrin found herself clenching her fists.

Sadira stepped between them. "I know you don't really believe she cheated," she said, "because that would mean you were also accusing our teachers of being fools for letting it happen. You are disappointed at coming in third because you are usually at the top, but this is better. Now everyone will be excited to see who will be on top next! Farrin has moved so far up in a single term that other girls will believe they can advance too. It will be better for our class to be excited. Better for the school, too, because other classes will want to see if they can beat us. And it will be better for the revolution, because the people will be served by well educated women."

Pargol squared her shoulders. "I can accept this talk about the revolution from you because you have paid for your words. You've lost family to the war and you live humbly. But this one," she jerked her thumb at Farrin, "is not about serving the people. She is about serving herself. Her whole family is selfish. They live in a mansion, thinking they can hide their guilt behind high walls. She even has a grandfather who was best buddies with the Shah!"

Another gasp from the students.

"We can't choose our relatives," Sadira said, keeping her voice quiet and steady. "Any family tree is bound to have a few rotten pomegranates."

"The whole point of the revolution was to bring an end to the rot," Pargol said, "not to make friends with it."

The group went tomb-silent. There was such meanness in the insult. It had gone beyond ordinary nastiness into something more sinister.

Farrin's heart began to thump in her chest.

Then she felt Sadira's hand slide gently into the bend of her elbow. Sadira guided her away.

"It's a beautiful day," Sadira said, softly, "and we are on top of the world."

Farrin put her hand on top of Sadira's.

She felt the ridge of Sadira's fingertips along her arm, and slowly she began to calm down.

Ten

The day was wine-glorious.

Farrin did not know where the phrase had come from or how it popped into her head. She did not drink wine. She had seen the way alcohol affected the adults around her and she never wanted to be that dull.

But still, the phrase fit.

The day was wine-glorious, and Farrin's heart was singing with joy.

She was heading down the highway on a bright sunny day, leaving her mother behind.

Life just kept getting better and better.

Her father sat beside Ahmad in the front seat. Farrin was in the backseat.

They were driving south out of Tehran, sometimes crawling in traffic, sometimes zipping along the highway and breezing through the checkpoints. A strong wind had blown much of the pollution away the night before. The air felt clean, the sky was blue, and Farrin's mother was back at home, nursing a bad headache.

Everyone knew her mother had no headache. Or, if she did, it was a medical marvel of a headache that only showed up once a year, when it was time to visit the in-laws.

"I won't be good company," her mother always said. "You go ahead and enjoy yourselves. Give my regards to your parents. I'll just take my pills and spend the day in a dark room."

Farrin knew her mother would do nothing of the sort. Her father knew it too. He knew what his wife thought of his family. She was probably going to spend the day with one of her boyfriends. His wife didn't know that he knew, and neither of them suspected that Farrin knew.

Secrets. Secrets everywhere.

Farrin didn't care.

Years ago, the last time her mother came on the annual trip, she had spent the whole time looking pained. She'd made a great show out of swatting away flies, refusing to eat, and putting a perfumed cloth to her nose to block out the smell of the livestock.

Farrin loved that her mother wasn't with them.

But the very best part of the day was that Sadira was sitting right next to Farrin in the backseat.

Farrin had arranged it all the week before, getting permission from Sadira's father and presenting the idea to her own father in a way that she knew he would not refuse.

"Sadira wants to learn more about the traditional way of life," Farrin told him.

"She is an interesting girl, this friend of yours," her father said. Although he built modern houses and his style of living was modern, he thought of himself as a traditional man. Watching her father meet Sadira's father, when they stopped to pick her up on the way out of Tehran, Farrin was reminded of this again. Her own dad had seemed almost jealous as he looked around the spartan yet restful front room of Sadira's house.

"Have you been to Shiraz?" she asked her friend, who had been silently watching the world go by through the car window.

"When I was small, I think," Sadira said. "Not that I remember."

"You'll like it," Farrin said. "It's beautiful." Like you, she almost added.

Sadira *was* beautiful, and they were going to have two whole days together without school getting in the way. They would visit Farrin's family the first day, and the second would be spent in the gardens, shrines, and coffee shops of one of Iran's oldest cities.

"Are you girls all right back there?"

Her father turned around in the passenger seat. "You're so quiet, I thought you might have both jumped out the window!"

Farrin was mortified by her father's attempt at humor, but Sadira handled it with grace.

"I've been marveling at how big Tehran has become," she said. "We learned in history class that it started as a village that grew pomegranates. Now it covers all this land!"

"You like to study history?" Farrin's father asked Sadira. "Well, let me tell you a thing or two about Iranian history."

Her father launched into a monologue about how Tehran's population grew in the thirteenth century, when prisoners escaped execution by the Mongols and ran away to settle in the area. Her father had not gone far in school, but he read a lot and he remembered what he read.

"Before that, they lived in underground houses—very clever, our ancestors! Being under the ground protected them from the heat in summer and the cold in winter."

That got her father started on his ideas of new kinds of buildings that could be developed for Iran, a blend of traditional wisdom and new technology. "Iran could be a world leader in housing design," he said.

Sadira sat through it all and even asked polite and appropriate questions.

"And then there is the whole developing area of solar power," her father said.

"We're here," said Ahmad.

They had turned from the highway onto a dirt track that became less of a road the farther they drove. The road ended at the bottom of a gently rounded hill. Ahmad parked the car beside an assortment of pickup trucks, motorbikes, and horse carts. Everyone got out.

Loaded down with boxes and baskets of food and gifts, they were just a few steps up the hill when a child's voice called out, "They're here!"

From that moment on, and for the rest of the afternoon,

Farrin felt like she was whirling in happy chaos.

Her father's whole extended family was there—aunts, uncles, sisters of aunts, grandparents, spouses, and so many cousins that Farrin could not keep up with all the names.

Everyone was happy to see her. Everyone welcomed Sadira as if she were part of the family.

Sadira made herself right at home, sitting with the women, playing with the new babies, helping to prepare the food, and learning how to clean wool and spin it with a hand spindle.

"Your friend has a glow about her," Farrin's grandmother said. She and Farrin were sitting together in the shade of a tent flap. Her grandmother was showing her a new embroidery stitch. "She'll make a good mother."

Farrin laughed. "We have to get through school first. Sadira came in first in the midterm scores."

"She's a smart girl, then," her grandmother said.

"Can I tell you a secret?" Farrin asked. "I came in second."

"You did? That's my girl!" Her grandmother gave her a hug. "Why is that a secret?"

"Mom doesn't want me to draw attention to myself," Farrin said, "because of who her family is."

"Go ahead and be proud. If your mother was thinking clearly, she would be proud of you too."

They all sat together for the evening meal on rugs spread out on the ground. The women sat on one side, and the men sat on the other.

Farrin sat beside Sadira on a rug made by her great-great-grandmother. The night sky was right above them. The good

Iranian ground was below them. They ate bread baked on hot stones and stew with goat meat and chickpeas. The air was full of laughter, storytelling, and music. Sadira played a tune on a santour the family provided. Everyone seemed to like her.

When there was a break in the music, Farrin's father turned to her grandfather and asked, "Is it getting easier for you? Are you being left alone?"

"It was bad under the Shah, and it is bad under the new government," her grandfather said. "I try to ignore all that. I have enough trouble with my goats and my sheep."

"I ask you this every year," her father said, "and I'm asking you again. Come and live with us. We have plenty of room. Or let me build you a house."

Farrin heard this exchange every year. She knew her grandfather would decline her father's offer. "There are more important things than comfort," he would say. "There are more important things than safety."

She didn't need to hear it again. She motioned to Sadira to follow her away from the crowd.

"Don't go too far, girls," her grandmother said. "There are sometimes wolves in these hills."

They stayed within sight of the family but went far enough away to have some privacy.

"I like your family," Sadira said.

"They like you too," said Farrin.

The moon rose over the trees. It was full and round. Its rays stroked Sadira's face, making it glow. The sight took Farrin's breath away.

Behind them, the family started up another song. The drums beat out something soft and ancient. The flute caught the breeze and the notes drifted close, then the wind shifted and the melody floated away again.

On top of the little hill, Farrin could see across into the valleys, where tiny villages and nomad camps sparkled with lanterns and cook fires.

She and Sadira were at the top of the world. They were floating above the smallness and fear and hatred and ugliness. There was no one around to put them down or hurt them or hold them back. There was just the world, the moon, and each other.

Farrin did not know what made her do it. There was no thought in her head of it before it happened. Her body moved without letting her mind know what it was doing.

She turned slightly toward Sadira. Sadira had already turned slightly toward her. Their heads moved close together, and, for the softest, slightest, most heavenly of moments, their lips touched in a kiss.

Then they just sat and watched the moon move across the sky. They did not speak. The moon spoke for them.

Eleven

Sounds of the morning filtered into the tent.

They were cheerful sounds—of children playing and others doing light work. The scents of wood smoke mingled with the scents of the animal skins that made up the tent and the musty smell of the old wool blanket wrapped around Farrin. She kept her eyes closed for a while longer, wanting to stretch out this moment.

Farrin always slept well when she visited her grandparents. Maybe it was the fresh air. Maybe it was the novelty of sharing her sleeping space with a bunch of other women and children, all cozy on rugs and mats.

Slowly, Farrin started to wake up. She could feel someone close beside her and she knew it was Sadira. Everyone else had already left the tent. She buried her face in Sadira's hair, breathing in the slight scent of jasmine. Her arms were around Sadira, and Sadira's arms were around her.

There was no better place in the world.

"You two had better hurry before all the food is—"

Farrin's grandmother stood over Farrin and Sadira, looking down at the way they were together.

The look on her grandmother's face made them pull apart.

"Good morning, Grandmother," Farrin said, trying to sound like she normally would. "Did you have a good sleep?"

She kept her hand in Sadira's. She didn't think to move it.

Her grandmother closed the tent flap and came close to them so that she could speak quietly.

"I have been told that your mother is dead," she said to Sadira. To Farrin, she said, "And your mother is..." There was no need to finish that sentence. "So perhaps no one has spoken to you about such things."

"What things, Grandmother?"

"You two are friends. Fine. That is a good thing. But make sure your friendship is just a friendship. Don't make it into something unnatural, something ugly. You should not hold onto each other like that. No man will want to marry you if you act like that with another girl. Don't do it! Your future will be crushed! This time, fine, you didn't know. There should not be another time. That is my message to you. Now you have heard it, there is no more need to talk about it." She headed out of the tent, saying over her shoulder, "Breakfast is ready."

She left them alone.

"I guess we'd better get up," Farrin said.

They got up from the mats and began to fold their blankets.

"She looked mad," Sadira said. "I'm sorry about that. I don't want your grandmother to be mad at you."

They folded the rest of the blankets in silence, and tidied up the other beds.

Just before they left the tent, Farrin turned to Sadira and said, "I'm not sorry."

They smiled at each other and went out into the day.

When they joined the others, all was the same as it was the night before. Farrin's father was in a great mood, women were busy with little tasks, and the men were already settled into smoking and talking.

Farrin and Sadira joined different groups of women doing different things. Sadira sat with the women milking goats, getting a lesson. Farrin helped the women chopping vegetables.

She looked up from her pile of onions to see her grandmother and father deep in conversation away from the others. She couldn't hear what they were saying, but she watched her dad gesture with his arms and his mother gesture back. When they both turned to look at her, she quickly glanced away.

Soon after, they all got back in the car and drove away.

Inside the car, the quiet seemed uneasy. The girls looked at each other across the backseat, but neither felt like talking.

This whole trip is going to be ruined, Farrin thought. She had to ask.

"Is everything all right?"

After a long silence her father sighed and said, "No. Your grandmother is mad at me."

"Why?"

"She wanted me to agree to a marriage for you with a cousin's son. I refused. So she's mad."

"She found a husband for me?"

"She said it was my duty as your father to get you locked into a marriage, and if I wasn't going to do it, then she would. I told her no. So, she's angry. But that's better than the alternative."

"Which boy was it? Was he creepy?"

"The boy seemed fine," her father said. "Serious, hard-working. I had nothing against the boy. No, it's better to have *my* mother angry at me than *your* mother angry at me. Can you imagine your mother's reaction if I arranged a marriage for you without her input—and to someone from my side of the family? No. I see my mother once a year, twice at most. I can live with her anger. But your mother is hard enough to live with as it is."

Relieved, Farrin grinned at Sadira.

Her father laughed. "We are on a holiday, are we not? So, let's have a good time. Ahmad, my good man, see if you can find anything worth listening to on the radio."

Ahmad picked up a Turkish music station and cranked up the volume. They sped off down the highway, and it was a holiday once again.

When they arrived in Shiraz, Ahmad parked the car near Azadi Park.

"I have business to attend to," her father said. "Ahmad will come with me. Can I trust the two of you to enjoy yourselves and be back here by two o'clock? It's a long drive back to Tehran."

"I know my way around," Farrin reminded him. "We'll stay in the center of the city."

He pointed to a statue surrounded by flower gardens and benches. "We will meet back at those benches," he said. He handed Farrin some money. "Have a nice lunch and a good time."

The girls climbed out of the car and watched the men drive off.

"We're free," Farrin said. "We're on our own in a strange city, and we have money to spend—we can do anything!" She took hold of Sadira's hand and they headed across the Esfahan Gate Bridge and into the old city.

Shiraz was beautiful, just as Farrin remembered it. The gardens were in bloom, the coffee houses were crowded with people enjoying the day, and the shops were full of books and clothes and pretty things to look at.

There was too much to see to waste time sitting in a restaurant for lunch, so they bought snacks from the street vendors and ate while they walked. They topped it off with saffron ice-cream cones, then headed to the Tomb of Hafez.

"I can't believe I'm really here," Sadira said. "I've been reading his poems ever since I first learned to read. And now I'm here."

Pools and gardens surrounded the carved marble pavilion. Underneath the archway, a large book was open on a pedestal. One by one, visitors to the shrine went up to the book, closed it and opened it again at random. They bent down closely to read what it said.

"Shall we do the faal-e Hafez?" Farrin suggested. "I've always wanted to, but the other times I was here it never seemed right."

They got into the line of people waiting to learn their future.

There was an old belief that, if you opened a volume of Hafez at random, particularly at his shrine, closed your eyes, and put your finger down on a page, the words would reveal what the future held.

The girls watched the others ahead of them, reading and reacting to the words. Some seemed happy, others confused. One woman appeared quite upset by what she read, and scuttled away.

When it came to their turn, Sadira suggested, "Let's do it together. I want to be your friend always, so let's see what the future holds for us both."

They closed the heavy volume. Then, with both hands on the book, they opened it. Eyes closed, hands clasped, fingers pointed, they plunged their hands together into the text of the great poet.

"You read it," Sadira said.

Farrin bent down to see the words better.

> "'No death invades a heart that comes alive in love:
> Our immortality is etched in the book of life.'"

She straightened up again.

"Those are the most beautiful words I have ever read," she said.

They didn't talk much after that. They wandered into the

garden behind the shrine and sat surrounded by flowers and birds, by people reading on benches, and by families having picnics in the grass. The day was calm and peaceful.

"The rest of our lives could be like this," Farrin said. "We could be together and work hard and then, whenever we get the chance, sit on a bench in a garden and just be quiet."

"That would be the best life," Sadira said. "We don't have to marry. We will qualify for places at a university, and then we will be professionals, earning our own money. We won't be bothering anyone. It will be a very lucky life."

They stayed in the garden as long as they could, then had to hurry back to the park to meet Farrin's father.

Ahmad and her father were waiting for them. "We finished our meeting early. Don't worry—you are not late. Did you have a good time?"

Back in the car, they headed out of Shiraz. Traffic was heavy, and they moved quite slowly.

"Take the next turn," her father told Ahmad. "We'll go through the village and pick up the highway north of here. Maybe this traffic jam will have cleared up by then."

They turned off the highway. The golden rocks and sand were broken up here and there with small nomad camps and shepherds with their flocks of sheep. Small market stalls along the road turned into small homes, then into slightly bigger homes as they neared the village.

Ahmad turned a corner, and then they saw the crowd.

"Turn around," Farrin's father said. "I don't know what this is, and I don't want to know."

Ahmad tried to make a three-point turn on the narrow country roadway, but the car behind him would not give him enough room. An oncoming car boxed them in so that their vehicle was stuck in the road sideways, with no room to go anywhere.

Farrin's father left the car to direct traffic, but it was no use. Speeding up the side of the road came one of the white trucks belonging to the Revolutionary Guard. The guardsmen jumped off the back of the truck and started ordering people out of their cars. One of them pointed his rifle right at Farrin's face through the window.

"Girls, get out of the car and stand with your father," Ahmad said. "Do what the soldiers tell you. Move easy, now. Nothing sudden."

Both girls got out Farrin's side of the car. They joined the others who were hustled along the side of the road and into the village. Farrin's father put a protective arm around both girls.

"What's going on?" Farrin asked him.

"Keep quiet," her father said. "Don't do anything to draw attention to yourself. They haven't told us that we're under arrest, so let's just do what they say and keep calm."

The Revolutionary Guard marched everyone to the village square. Farrin's father guided the girls to a spot in the crowd where they could stand behind taller people and not be seen. Farrin checked her head covering to be sure no hair was showing, although the guards appeared to be focused on something else.

A construction crane sat in the middle of the square. Around it, the guardsmen waited. They were dressed all in black and hooded, with masks covering their faces.

Farrin reached for Sadira's hand and squeezed it.

She couldn't see, but she heard the crowd go quiet. Several of the guards shouted something through their megaphones, but the sound was so muffled, Farrin couldn't make out what they were saying.

And then the crane jerked upward. On the end of the line, where there should have been a wrecking ball, was a man.

His hands were bound behind his back, his legs were tied together, and his face was uncovered so that everyone could witness the agony of his last gasps for breath. He swung and twisted on the wire. In a futile attempt to escape the tightening of the noose, he jerked his legs and tried to spin himself away. Two jerks, three, five. Farrin lost count.

It took the man many long minutes to die.

The Revolutionary Guardsmen made more indecipherable speeches through their megaphones, then they let the crowd go. Her father led Farrin and Sadira away.

It was a relief to get back inside the car. After a short period of confusion, the cars sorted themselves out and they were back on the road again.

Sadira gripped Farrin's hand all the way back to Tehran.

Twelve

"'Don't be more than others
So I urge my heart...'"

It was Rumi Day at school.

The youngest junior class was up on stage, reciting a few short verses. Their eyes were glued to their teacher, a smiling young woman who encouraged them every time they fumbled the words.

Farrin's school put a lot of emphasis on math and science, expecting that many of its students would go on to study medicine.

"But knowledge without appreciation for culture creates only half a person," Principal Kobra was fond of saying to new parents as she toured them through the school. "Your child will know her Ferdowsi, Rumi, and Hafez as well as her multiplication tables."

Once a term, the school displayed its poetic knowledge. Parents and officials were invited. Farrin's father had to work and she hadn't bothered to ask her mother, so neither of them was there.

Sadira's father wasn't there, either. "He already knows I can recite poetry," she said.

The presenters grew in size, and the length of their recitations increased. Farrin became more and more nervous as the time approached for her class to present.

She had been assigned a long poem about Solomon meeting with the birds and understanding all their words even though the birds had so many different calls. The message of the poem was about how it was possible to communicate the important things even if there are different languages involved. It was a long poem, but Farrin was not worried about that. Learning something by memory was simply a matter of concentration. She could recite the poem backward and forward.

But she was still worried because the poem she had been assigned was not the poem she was going to present.

In the days following the Shiraz trip, something had become very clear to Farrin.

She was in love with Sadira.

There was no other explanation for it. Sadira was the first thought in her head when she opened her eyes in the morning and the last thought she had before she fell asleep. Every evening at nine o'clock she went outside to look up at the moon, blow it a kiss, and whisper secrets for it to deliver to her friend.

When she was in a room without Sadira, the room felt empty. When Sadira was with her, no matter how crowded the room was, no one else was there.

And no matter how much time they spent together, it never felt like enough.

Farrin had been trying to get up the nerve to tell Sadira how she felt. Sometimes when they studied together, she came close to a confession, but then Sadira would ask for help with a trigonometry problem or ask if she could remember the source of the Euphrates River. They would talk about schoolwork and Farrin would get tongue-tied about the important things—and not be able to say it.

Today, she was determined. She was going to do it in front of everyone, in a way that would make it absolutely clear how she felt and how happy she was about it.

After that, she could worry about whether or not Sadira felt the same way.

She was going to do it in a poem.

At first she tried to write her own poem, but nothing she could write described the ache and joy of what she felt for Sadira. She went looking through the classics, and in the end came back to Rumi.

But not a Rumi poem ever assigned at school.

Her class was called. She walked with them up to the stage and stood in rehearsed formation for the choral reading.

When that was done, she stepped forward. It was her turn now.

She walked to the center of the stage, right down to the front. Her tiptoes, in their shined black oxfords, hung over the edge of the platform.

She looked right at Sadira's face and began to recite.

"'Exquisite love, what exquisite love we have,
How fine, how good, how beautiful,
How warm, how warm, this sunlight love keeps us
How hidden, hidden, but how real…'"

Sadira's eyes were shining and she was smiling.

"'… Once more, and again once more,
what mad passion is this …'"

The door to the gymnasium banged open. A dozen members of the Revolutionary Guard, their guns pointed, stomped through the crowd of students.

The girls' shrieks were cut off as the soldiers pushed them aside with their rifles and shouted at them to be quiet.

"What right do you have to come bursting in here?"

Principal Kobra strode up to the commanding officer and brushed aside his rifle as if it were no more powerful than a wooden ruler.

"We go where we choose," the officer said. "We don't explain ourselves to you."

"Watch your tone," Principal Kobra said. "This is a school. These are my students. I am their principal. If you want to speak to them, you will go through me."

The guardsmen ignored her and marched onto the stage.

Farrin was too shocked to move. One of her classmates pulled her back to rejoin the others.

The commander of the guardsmen spoke in a loud voice. "I want the student who is responsible for this."

He pulled out of his pocket a folded sheet of paper, opened

it, and held it out. It was one of the women's rights pamphlets that had been floating around.

"We have been informed that a student from this school has done this. I want to know who it is, and I want to know now."

Principal Kobra came up on stage.

"I am the principal," she said again. "Leave this with me. I will find the culprit and turn her over to the authorities. There are young children here and you are scaring them."

The commanding officer shoved Principal Kobra so hard she fell to the stage floor. Farrin was the closest. Without thinking, she helped the principal to her feet.

The commander spoke again.

"I ask again, who is responsible for this?"

No one came forward.

"Nobody will answer me? Then I will decide for myself who is responsible."

He spun around and looked at the group behind him on stage. He walked up close to each one, looking into her face intently before moving on to the next one. When he came to Farrin, he stopped.

"You were the one who picked up your principal," he said. "Did you write this pamphlet? Did you write, 'Iranian women overthrew the Shah only to be betrayed by the Ayatollah?'"

Farrin was too frightened to speak. The commander was bigger, louder, and meaner than anyone she had ever encountered before. She could not open her mouth to speak.

"Take her," he said to his guards.

Two guards grabbed Farrin's arms and dragged her off the stage.

Farrin struggled but there was no escaping the grip they had on her. She heard Sadira cry out. She heard the teachers pull students out of the way. She heard the principal argue with the commander.

And then she heard another voice.

"I wrote the pamphlet!"

This voice was so loud and so strong, it rose above the others.

The soldiers hauling Farrin stopped and turned around.

Standing in the center of the stage was Rabia, Head Girl of the school.

The students froze.

"I wrote the pamphlet," Rabia repeated. "I wrote it and typed it and printed it myself. No one helped me. I am responsible for it, and I stand by every word in it. My mother fought for the revolution and she—"

Whatever else Rabia was going to say next was lost as the guards engulfed her.

Farrin heard a few stray words as Rabia was dragged away, words like "Freedom" and "Fight for rights."

Rabia was popular. The crowd surged forward to follow her. The girls ignored their teachers' attempts to keep them out of the Revolutionary Guards' way. In the confusion, the guards holding onto Farrin released their grip. In that instant, Farrin was yanked away and swallowed up by the student body. She became just one more school uniform in a sea of others.

Farrin found Sadira. They made it outside, but it was too late.

Rabia had been taken away.

Thirteen

Trigonometry had lost its appeal.

Farrin and Sadira sat on the floor, their books spread out before them as usual, but neither could study.

After Rabia's arrest, the girls had been led back to their classrooms. The Rumi Day assembly was over. The rest of the morning had gone on as usual.

The teachers had tried to resume lessons, but Farrin doubted that anyone had listened. Finally at lunchtime, Farrin and Sadira had escaped to the privacy of the gym.

"What will they do to her?" Farrin wondered. She was thinking of the village, where they watched the man swing from the crane.

"They don't hang girls, do they?" Sadira asked, voicing Farrin's thoughts. "They wouldn't do that, just because she wrote something."

"How does that pamphlet hurt the country?" asked Farrin

in return. "The government says education is important, but if they educate us, then we will start to think. And if we start to think, then we will have opinions."

"They won't hang her," said Sadira. "I'm sure they won't hang her, or even torture her, like they did to my father. They'll probably just lecture her and scare her a little. It wouldn't make sense for them to hang her. Rabia's really smart. Iran needs smart women."

The girls picked up their trigonometry books again and pretended to study. They pretended it was an ordinary day and they had a class to prepare for.

Farrin stared at the page but could take nothing in. She was about to ask Sadira if she was having the same problem when the other girl spoke.

"What was that poem you were reciting? Weren't you supposed to do the one about the birds?"

Farrin put her textbook back on the floor.

"It sounded like a good poem," Sadira said. "At least the bit you were able to get out before the guard came in. Do you know the rest of it?"

"I know all of it," said Farrin.

"Feel like giving me a private recitation?"

The floor of the gym was not the right place. Farrin got to her feet and held out her hand. She pulled Sadira up and led her to the stage, where she found a high stool for her friend to perch on. Then Farrin stood before her and recited.

The poem came from her lips with all the love and passion she felt but had not been able to express. When it was done,

Sadira rose from the stool and took Farrin's hand.

As though they were speaking with one mind, one heart, one voice, they said together and with the same sense of wonder, "I love you."

And they embraced.

Farrin was floating ten miles in the sky above Tehran. Sadira loved her! This wonderful, beautiful, heavenly girl loved *her!* She wanted to dance and sing and leap from mosque tower to mosque tower, proclaiming from every loudspeaker in Iran that Sadira loved her and she loved Sadira.

They were still kissing when they heard the door slam.

They had thought they were alone.

But someone had seen.

I feel too happy to care, Farrin thought.

And she kissed Sadira again.

FOURTEEN

"I saw them."

Of course it was Pargol. It had to be her, on monitor duty, checking out all the places where students might go to get into trouble without being seen. Sometimes she caught students with illegal fashion magazines. Sometimes she caught juniors, their heads bare, wearing their hijabs like capes or backwards for a game of Blind Girl's Bluff. Sometimes she didn't catch anybody doing anything wrong, so she made things up, like, "Don't you know this area is off-limits to students on Tuesdays? Get out. The next time you're caught here, you'll go on report."

"We were doing our trigonometry prep," Sadira said. "We're allowed to study in the gym. There's lots of room to spread out our books, and it's quiet, so we can study without interruption."

"You were not studying," said Pargol.

"We were taking a short break," Farrin said. "Sadira wanted to hear the poem I started to recite at the assembly. So, just to stretch our legs a bit, we went up on stage. It was a poem by Rumi," she added, "because it was Rumi Day."

She directed this last bit to her mother and father, who were sitting in uncomfortable chairs in Principal Kobra's office. Sadira's father was also there. His chair was slightly more comfortable, but he did not look any happier than Farrin's parents.

"It was disgusting, what I saw," Pargol said. "The sort of thing that should never happen between two girls. They are freaks."

Farrin was shocked to hear her mother speak up. "My daughter is not a freak. Farrin has been attending this school for years. I attended this school when I was a girl, before—well, before. I don't know where your monitor comes from, but I can assure you, if any girl here is a freak, it's certainly not *my* daughter."

Her mother was not helping.

Her mother would be angry at being forced to come back to a place she considered to be taken over by savages and peasants. She would also be mad at Farrin for drawing attention to herself when she had been so often ordered not to.

Farrin's father was also looking furious. He had not looked up at her once since entering the principal's office.

Farrin could deal with her parents' anger, especially her mother's; it was an everyday event at her house.

But there was something more that made her afraid, and

it was related to what her grandmother had said. Was she about to be crushed?

"May I ask what arrangements have been made for them once they graduate?" Principal Kobra asked.

"You mean, what university will Farrin apply to?" her father asked.

"She means a husband," snapped Farrin's mother. "She wants to know if we have arranged her marriage yet. Tell her it's none of her business."

"You can speak to me yourself," Principal Kobra said. "I'm sitting right in front of you. I suggest that if you have not made marriage arrangements already, then you should do it quickly. And if a marriage has been arranged, I suggest you consider moving up the date. They are smart girls. The right marriages will protect them from unnatural tendencies. They might even continue their educations. I could arrange for them to take accelerated studies so they would be ready to sit their final exams in a few months. Then they could graduate high school before their marriages."

Farrin started to panic at this. There was too much going on in that small room, and none of it was in her control.

Would Sadira's father force her to marry? Her own parents would not really make her get married, would they? They were so modern and Western in their thinking. Hadn't her father been mad at her grandmother for suggesting a husband for Farrin?

Sadira was standing by her father, her head down. Farrin vowed then and there that she would do everything in her power to keep any marriages from happening. She and Sadira were in love. They were supposed to be together.

We'll run away, Farrin thought. *I'll steal money from my mother and make Ahmad drive us to Turkey.*

She pictured the two of them riding horses across the desert, crossing the border at night on foot, creeping silently so they would not alert the border guards.

She was so caught up in her vision that the principal's voice took her by surprise.

"We cannot have this sort of thing happening at our school," Principal Kobra said. "There are already men in the community who think that by teaching our girls to be smart and confident, we have turned them into immodest troublemakers. If word gets around that we've allowed this kind of immorality to flourish, we will all be in trouble."

"Immorality?" Farrin asked, speaking up even though she knew that it would be better to keep her mouth shut. "We're in love. We're not hurting anybody. I don't see how this is anybody's business but our own."

"I really should expel them both," Principal Kobra said, ignoring Farrin, "but they are top students and could have excellent futures. Perhaps this is just a childish phase they are going through. So, I will permit them to stay for the next few months in an accelerated program. But they are on probation. Any further incident and it will be out of my hands."

"You're not going to report them?" This came from Pargol, who looked almost physically ill with disappointment.

"No, I am not," said the principal. "And let me say now,

before all of you, how very grateful I am to Pargol for bringing this matter to our attention. I don't know how the school would function without the eyes and ears of my monitors. Pargol, I have a further task for you."

Pargol stood up straighter. "Anything, Principal Kobra."

"I want you to deputize some of your classmates. I know you cannot watch them all the time. You have your own studies and personal business to attend to. So I want you to put together a brigade of students who will take turns keeping an eye on Farrin and Sadira. And if there are any transgressions, I want to know immediately. Can you do that for me?"

"Yes, of course, Principal Kobra."

"Thank you. Farrin and Sadira, this is my decision. You will continue to attend this school. You will continue to make excellent grades. Other than in matters of academics in the classroom, you will not speak to each other, you will not meet each other, and you will not study together. Frankly, with the study program I will create for you, you won't have time for anything but your schoolbooks. You will absolutely never be alone together again. Do you understand? Tell me you agree right now or I will expel you immediately."

They did not have much choice. "Yes, Principal Kobra," Farrin said.

Sadira just nodded her agreement.

"I want to emphasize that the consequences of further transgressions will be much more severe than simple expulsion and the end of your academic futures. This sort of activity is against the natural order and will be seen as an act of treachery against the common good. I do hope you are hearing me on this. Are there any questions?"

No one had any questions. With a wave of the principal's hand, everyone was dismissed

Without looking up, Sadira walked away with her father.

Farrin didn't have the courage to call after her.

The ride back to Farrin's house was like riding home in a knot that got tighter and tighter the closer they were to home. By the time they arrived at the house, Farrin felt as if she were trapped in a vice.

Her mother followed Farrin up to her bedroom but did not speak until the door was closed behind them.

"I always knew there was something wrong with you," she said. "I just never imagined it would be this. All we have given you, all we have done for you—and this is how you pay us back? I should let your father go ahead and marry you off to that monkey nephew of his, and you can go live among the goats and be somebody else's problem. I should just go ahead and let that happen. It would be better for us if you were dead. How can I explain this to my family? And your father—I know you don't think much of me, but you can't even behave yourself for your father's sake? You are a monster and a freak, and if you do anything more—*anything*—to bring shame and attention on this family, I will wash my hands of you. I'm not even going to ask you if you understand. You're a smart girl. You understand."

With that, her mother left the room and closed the door. A moment later, Ada brought in some boxes and packed up all Farrin's videotapes, music cassettes, and books. She took everything out with her and did not look at Farrin once.

Farrin was left alone.

She went to her bed. And cried.

That night she sat by the window. She could not see the moon at nine, but she knew it was there, and she hoped Sadira had not forgotten.

Fifteen

Dear Farrin:

I hope you will forgive me for writing this letter. It is going against the rule that forces us apart. But it is not a good rule! If I cannot at least be in touch with you through pen and paper, all I see for my life is desolation.

I don't know when—or if—you will get this note. How often do you check your storage bin in the cloakroom? And I will fold it until it is a tiny piece of paper. You could easily miss it—or worse. You could mistake it for scrap and throw it away.

But I do not believe this will happen. I believe that the love I feel for you has spread from my heart into the ink of my pen. That love will draw you to this note—you will not be able to ignore it.

If you do not want to respond, I understand. It is a big risk. If you no longer love me, then all hope is gone, and I will resign myself to darkness. I will still treasure every moment I spent knowing you.

I love you. This love brings only joy to me. No matter what happens next.

All my love,
Sadira

Dearest Sadira:

Your letter did draw me to it—how brave you were to write it! How lovely you are and how strong. Your love for me is a miracle, one that I am thankful for every day.

These days I have a lots of time to think. The house is silent. My parents had our housekeeper take away all the things I used to think were entertaining—my television, my tapes of *The Night Stalker*, my books, my radio, my cassette player. They did this to punish me, I know. But they really did me a favor.

All I have now is my book about demon hunting and my memories of you. If that is all I ever have in my life, it is enough. But I am not yet ready to bow down to the demons that run the world!

Know, my love, that I am always looking out for you. We will find a way…

Love,
Farrin

Dearest Farrin:

Pargol's little Tikes of Terror are taking great pleasure in not letting me out of their sight for one single second! I have tried several times to get notes to you, but every time I think I have a clear moment, another clutch of Pargol's juniors comes out of nowhere.

They laugh and skip around me and say, "Where are you going, Sadira? Are you going to see Farrin?" Their questions make me feel shame, as though I've done wrong. But the better part of me knows we have done nothing to be ashamed of. They are too young to understand what it will do to them, this spying on others in hopes of ratting them out. I fear for the future of their characters. I fear for the future of Iran.

We have hurt no one. We have done nothing against the state or the revolution. If two girls who love each other threaten the revolution, then it isn't worth much. Time for a new revolution!

I *will* get this note to you! I *will!*

Love,
Sadira

PS: When you hear me cough three times, I am saying, "I love you."

My lovely Sadira:

Watching Pargol made Head Girl this morning disgusted me. The only good thing about that whole awful assembly was when you managed to get close to me as we filed out of the gym.

How much I long to hug you! I have the memory, but I don't want it to be only in my past. I want a future with you, too.

There must be a way to let people know we are serious and just want to be together. I have thought of several ways that we could protest what has been done to us, but there is a problem with each idea—

We could go on a hunger strike. I discounted this idea quickly, since I'm not sure anyone would notice. If they did notice, I'm not sure they would care.

We could refuse to study. This idea is also no good. Our parents would just decide to marry us off faster. If we don't graduate we will have fewer choices, no matter what sort of life we end up with.

We could appeal to someone. Where would we go to do this? Who has the power to keep us together without hating us for loving each other? There is no one who will help us.

We could run away. There. I've said it. I don't know how we would do it, but I think we should find a way to leave Tehran and maybe even Iran. I don't know where we could go, but there must be some place where people will leave us alone. They wouldn't have to like us. As long as they let us be.

By the way, as a final, insulting exercise of power, my parents took away my demon-hunting book. All my notebooks are gone. All burned. They really don't like anything about me.

All my love,
Farrin

PS: Three little coughs—the most sublime music in the world!

Dear Farrin:

I have also thought of all the things you have thought of, and come to the same conclusion. We can shout, but no one will listen. We can starve ourselves, but no one will notice. We can refuse to study, but we will hurt only ourselves.

Maybe we could disappear. Maybe no one would mind. They might even be happy to be rid of us. My father already treats me as if I am dead. Why is it anybody's business if we want to leave? We have no children, no husbands, no responsibilities. Why should anyone care if we want to live together?

But these are the thoughts of a child. We cannot afford to be children.

I don't know why it is anybody's business, but it is. And if we are caught trying to leave, I have a feeling that it will go very bad for us.

I can't see any way out. If we leave, they will find us. If we stay, we are doomed.

Loving you was still worth it.

Love,
Sadira

PS: Too bad about your book. I hope you will get a chance to rewrite it.

My dear Sadira:

I hate that you are so sad and so downhearted. You are nothing but light and music and jasmine and all things good. There should never be a shadow over you. There should not even be the barest hint of a bitter wind touching your gentle face.

I saw our moon at nine o'clock. It should have made me happy, but it seemed cold and cruel, as if it were taunting us because we cannot be together.

I need to see you. These notes are too risky and haphazard. What if they fall into the wrong hands? It is only by chance that you were chosen to hand out the physics assignments yesterday, and that you had a note ready to slip to me when you passed my desk. I continue to be in awe of your courage.

What if I could arrange for us to meet, in secret? Would you risk it?

All my love,
Farrin

Dear Farrin:

I am so lonely! If only my mother were still alive, she would help me. I'm sure she would.

The academic studies that used to bring me joy now have the color of doom about them. Each completed lesson brings me closer to the end of whatever time I have left in the same building as you. I live for each glance of your face, for each time I hear your voice give an answer in class, for each group of three short coughs you give in answer to mine.

When we graduate, that will be the end. I will never see you again.

This understanding has finally sunk in.

If I never see you again, I might as well be dead.

So, yes, I will risk anything to see you.

Love,
Sadira

Dear Sadira:

For a while, after all this trouble started, my parents put a hold on their stupid social lives. But they are getting back into it. They don't like each other, and all those evenings with no one to talk to but each other is starting to drive them crazy.

I am as good as gold. I don't talk back to my mother. I stay out of my father's way (he still hasn't spoken to me). I do all my studies and I don't complain.

Maybe they are thinking they can forget about me again.

They are having one of their silly parties—the silliest one of the year—on October 31. Can you find a way to slip out of your home in the evening? I have persuaded Ahmad to pick you up and sneak you into my room. We can have a few hours to ourselves, and then he will take you back home before your father discovers you are gone.

What do you think?

Love,
Farrin

Dear Farrin:

My father pays so little attention to me now that I doubt he will even notice if I'm not there. He won't even eat with me. I have to prepare his meal, put it on a tray, and leave the room. Only then will he go to the kitchen, take the tray, and go to his own room to eat.

As you know, the only door to the house is in my father's room, but if I can get the screen off the window in my room, I will escape.

Tell me the time and the place where I should wait for Ahmad. I will be there. Even if it's only for a few hours, I will be filled with enough hope to keep going.

We are full human beings, you and I. We are not the property of our parents or our future husbands or the revolution or anybody. Sure, we are born into a country and a culture and a history and a society, and those things will always be a part of us.

But first and most important, we are human beings with a right to choose for ourselves how we want to live. All we have is our lives. Each person gets just one. We owe our parents and the revolution our respect, but we don't owe them everything. And everything is what they want.

I choose you, not just because you are wonderful and not just because you love me.

I choose you because the act of choosing you belongs to me. It is mine, my choice, my free will.

I choose you over my father. I choose you over my country.

And even if you decide you don't want me, I still choose you.

Because in choosing you, I am choosing myself.

Time and place, my darling. I'll be there.

All my love,
Sadira

SIXTEEN

"Happy Birthday!"

The crowd of adults in Farrin's inner living room raised their glasses to a photo of Reza Pahlavi, the crown prince of Iran, the eldest son of the Shah, and her mother's greatest hope for the future of civilization.

The prince has a tea stain on his collar, Farrin thought.

It was an old photograph. The prince was still a child in it. There used to be a piece of glass protecting the photo, but it was broken during the last birthday party. Someone who'd had too much to drink stumbled into the little table that held the photo and brought the whole thing crashing down. During the cleanup, cold tea was splattered on it.

Farrin was dressed up and passing around trays of finger foods. The recipe for the pinwheel sandwiches came from one of the old issues of *Ladies Home Journal*, brought to the house by the Briefcase Man. Everyone raved about how clever the little sandwiches were. Farrin tried one. It was nothing special.

She kept her eyes on the door as she passed the trays around.

Acting like the smiling, dutiful daughter was Farrin's way of trying to make it up to her parents, to prove to them that everything was back the way it was, back when she was too young to know that she could ask questions. Her mother seemed to accept that the obedient, nicely-brushed-up Farrin was the real Farrin. She ordered her around and did not seem at all surprised when Farrin did as she was told.

Farrin's father had not spoken to her since the day in the principal's office. Farrin stayed out of his way.

Even tonight, as he was standing with some of his business associates and sharing a joke, he did not acknowledge her when she offered a tray to the group. Farrin barely noticed the snub. She had other things to think about.

Every time the door to the inner room opened, it was just Ada with more food or a new guest arriving.

Something will go wrong, Farrin thought. She kept a smile on her face and a polite tone to her voice. *All you silly people, taking food from me and asking your vapid questions about school—what have any of you ever had to worry about? You have no idea that you are being served by a girl who is about to disobey her parents on a major scale, if all goes right—which it won't, it won't. She won't come. I won't see her.*

Then the door opened again, and Ahmad stepped inside.

The nod he gave to Farrin was so slight as to be imperceptible to everyone but her.

"Ahmad, is there a problem?"

Farrin's father came over to him.

"Sir, I just wanted you to know that the car is washed and ready for tomorrow."

"Of course it is," Farrin's father said. "That's your job. Anything else?"

"No, sir."

"Then don't hang about staring at the guests."

Ahmad left, closing the door behind him. Farrin busied herself with refilling her tray. She did not look up from the arrangement of small pastries, but she could tell her father was watching her. His shoes were on the floor just a few feet from her—she could see them out of the corner of her eye. They were pointing in her direction.

She kept rearranging the pastries, afraid that if she looked up her father would know she had a secret.

At last, one of his friends called him over and the shoes turned and walked away.

Farrin stayed in the room a while longer, chatting pleasantly and even playing a few song requests on the piano. Then, tired of Farrin hogging all the attention, her mother decided to make a speech, and Farrin took the opportunity to slip out of the room.

In a flash, she was up the stairs and inside her bedroom.

In the next second, she was wrapped in Sadira's arms.

They stood holding each other, not speaking, swaying slightly to the rhythm of their shared heartbeat.

"This is better," Sadira said.

"I have missed you so much," said Farrin. "I can't not be with you or talk to you. It's torture."

Someone rattled the doorknob and the girls jumped apart. Farrin knew the door was locked, but it gave her a scare.

"Is this the powder room?" a woman asked from the hallway.

"It's downstairs by the front door," Farrin called back.

"Farrin, dear, is that you? You are such a lovely girl. Such a blessing to your parents."

Farrin recognized the voice. "Thank you, Mrs. Hafezi. I'm going to bed now—I'm pretty tired."

"You get your beauty sleep, young lady," Mrs. Hafezi said, and then she laughed as if she had made a clever joke. The girls heard her laugh all the way down the stairs.

"Mrs. Hafezi is having a good night," Farrin said. "They are celebrating the birthday of the crown prince."

"He's not here, is he?" Sadira asked. "You told me your mom was a follower of the Shah, but to have the prince right here—"

Farrin laughed. "Don't worry. He went to the United States before the revolution. The prince is represented by a very old photograph with a tea stain. Nothing more counter-revolutionary than that."

Sadira sat on the edge of the bed. "I hope you won't be mad at me," she said.

"Mad at you?" Farrin sat beside her. "I never could be mad at you."

"You might be when you've heard what I've done."

Farrin was about to ask what Sadira was talking about when she looked over and saw a tote bag dropped alongside the wall by the bookshelf.

"I left," Sadira said. "I mean, I really left. I know the plan was for Ahmad to drive me back to school first thing in the morning, then come back and drive you, like nothing had ever happened. But I had to leave. My father has arranged a marriage for me. The wedding is set for next month. He isn't even going to let me graduate!"

Farrin sat beside Sadira and put an arm around her shoulder, drawing her close.

"My father hasn't spoken to me since that day in the principal's office," Sadira said. "Not a word. He's gone back to that sad place, but it's worse now. He doesn't even acknowledge me. It's like I'm a ghost in the house."

Farrin gently rocked her friend in her arms.

"I only found out about the wedding when I overheard him argue with Rabbi Sayyed. The rabbi tried to talk him out of it, but my father refused to listen. They argued—it was terrible! I've destroyed their friendship—another sin to add to my list."

Farrin was too busy thinking to respond to this.

"When will he notice that you have left?"

"Not until supper, when no food tray appears," Sadira said. "Maybe even later than that. Sometimes he eats all his meals out of the house, just to avoid me. Can you help me get out of Tehran? I hate to ask. I know you have your own troubles with your parents."

"If you're leaving, I'm leaving with you," Farrin said. She didn't even have to think about it. Of course they were going together!

Sadira threw her arms around Farrin and sobbed with relief. Farrin rubbed her shoulders to comfort her, but only for a moment. There was too much to do.

"We need a plan," Farrin said. "And money." She wondered how much money she had in her room. She knew where her mother kept a small stash of cash, to hand out to the poor or to pay for last-minute groceries, and she could probably get her hands on it after everyone left or went to bed. There wouldn't be much, though.

I'll have to take it directly from my parents, Farrin decided. She didn't like the thought of doing that.

They'd have to pay for her if she stayed, she reasoned. School supplies, clothes, food. And if they wanted to marry her off, they would have had to pay for that, too. Whatever she managed to take from them tonight would be less than it would cost them if she stayed.

She recognized that it was flimsy morality, but it would have to do. If they were going to get away, and have any kind of a life, they would need money—as much money as possible.

"I brought my gold," Sadira said, pointing to the thin gold chain around her neck.

Girls were often given pieces of gold jewelry for their birthdays and special occasions like New Year or Eid. This gold was to form part of their dowry when they married.

"Cash would be better," Farrin said, "but gold is good, too."

She got out the food and drinks she had prepared. They sat on the bed and ate and planned.

"I don't want to trust Ahmad with this," Farrin said. "He has been trustworthy so far, because he knows that I could report him to my father for taking food to the workers. But this is too big. We need to be able to get away without his help."

There were so many problems. Girls out alone did not draw too much attention if they were wearing school uniforms during the hours when they should be heading to or from school, but girls alone in regular clothes outside school hours would just be asking for the Revolutionary Guard to arrest them.

It would be hard to find a taxi driver willing to give them a ride. Even if they said they were sisters, the driver would want to know why they were traveling without their father or brother. There were checkpoints along the highway and at bus stations. Everywhere they went, too many people would ask too many questions.

They talked and talked. They went through Sadira's bag and Farrin's belongings, deciding what to take with them.

"Only what we can carry easily," Farrin said. "Maybe we shouldn't take anything except food, water, and money. We'll draw less attention if we're not carrying travel bags."

"Where should we go?" Sadira asked.

They went through the list of neighboring countries. Iraq? They were not likely to be made welcome there, and their knowledge of Arabic was limited to the Quran. Pakistan? They wouldn't blend in there at all. Afghanistan? There were a lot of Farsi speakers there, but there was also a civil war going on. Turkey? A lot of escaping Iranians went through there. If they could get into Turkey, they could cross over into Europe.

"Turkey," Sadira said. "That sounds best. Once we're in Turkey, we'll consider the next place."

They decided to wait until just before daylight to leave. In the coldest hours of the morning, the city would be in its deepest sleep, and they would have the best chance to walk without being seen. They could cover a lot of miles on the empty streets; and by the time the sun came up and the city awoke, they would be far away. On the bus, they might even blend in with the female university students, gaining even more distance.

Farrin unlocked her bedroom door and checked the hallway. Below, they were singing. Her parents' room was just down the hall. Moving quickly, she listened at the door before opening it. Some guests had been known to slip up there during parties. Tonight, Farrin did not hear anything.

Inside the room, she went to her mother's jewelry box and took a few small things that she didn't think her mother would miss. Some cash sat in the tray on the bureau. Farrin found more in the closet where her mother kept her purses. Farrin grabbed all she could find. She was tempted to do a more thorough search of the room, but she didn't want to leave Sadira alone too long.

She made it back to her room without being seen.

They put on two layers of clothing to avoid carrying them.

"This is good," Farrin said. "We might have to sleep outside sometimes. Now we will be warm enough."

Soon they had done all they could to get ready. Farrin set her alarm clock and they stretched on the bed to rest.

"I'll put the clock under my pillow," she said. "That way, we'll be able to hear it, but it won't be loud enough to wake up my parents."

She turned out the lamp. They lay side by side in the darkness with only the light from the moon to illuminate the room.

"There's our moon," Sadira said. "Should we take it with us when we leave?"

"It belongs to us," Farrin said. "We can't leave it behind."

They were quiet for a moment, then Farrin asked, "Are you scared?"

"I'm sad," Sadira said. "I'm happy to be with you, but I am sad to leave my father. He won't understand why I had to go. I don't want him to think I left because I thought he was a bad father. He's a good father. The man he arranged for me to marry is probably a kind man, because my father would want that for me. But I don't want to be married. I want to be with you."

"Everything will be all right," Farrin said. "Whatever happens, it will be all right."

They lay close together on the bed. Farrin pulled a blanket over them. "We should take a blanket with us," she said. "One each. We could wear them around our shoulders like shawls."

Sadira giggled. "Won't Pargol be mad to learn that we've gone?" she said. "Her spies will have nothing to do."

They talked quietly and laughed and held hands and stayed warm and close under the blanket. The moon moved across

Farrin's window, taking its rays from the room as the girls slid together into a calm, happy, dreamless sleep.

They were still asleep when the Revolutionary Guard burst through the bedroom door.

Seventeen

"We didn't do anything wrong."

Farrin's upper arms ached. The Revolutionary Guard women had such a strong grip on her that her lower arms were beginning to go numb.

"Stop talking," one of the guardswomen said. "We don't want to hear it."

"But you are making a mistake," insisted Farrin. "We are top students. We go to an academy for gifted girls and we are at the top of our class. Ask anyone at our school. How can anyone who is at the top of their class do anything wrong?"

In her head Farrin knew she wasn't making any sense. Of course people who were at the top of their class could also be people who had done wrong. But she was talking just to keep talking, as if talking alone could save her.

"We even have good grades in trigonometry," she said. "That's a really hard subject, so you know we have to do a lot of studying in order to get good grades. We have no time to get into trouble, so you clearly have the wrong people.

"I want to see my parents," she added. "Where are my parents?"

No one would answer her. While some of the guards held onto Sadira and Farrin, the others searched Farrin's bedroom.

Farrin tried to squirm away, but it was impossible. She twisted her head as far back as she could, but she could not see into the hall.

Sadira didn't squirm. She stood with her head hung low—as if she were still in the principal's office.

From below came the sounds of her mother giving the Revolutionary Guard a hard time.

"Why is a photograph illegal? How can a photo be against the law? By any standards of decency—"

Then Farrin heard her father's voice, lower and indecipherable, trying to calm her mother down.

The guardswomen must have received some sort of signal, because in the next instant Farrin and Sadira were hustled down the stairs and out of the house. Farrin looked around for her parents but she couldn't see them.

"I demand to see my father!" Farrin shouted. Perhaps if she acted like a big shot, the guardswomen would listen to her.

They didn't. Instead, Farrin and Sadira were surrounded by male soldiers, put into the back of a truck, and taken away into the night. Ordered to be silent, they were forced to sit facing away from each other as the truck sped down the streets—the same streets the girls had planned to take for their escape.

"I'm sorry we fell asleep," Farrin said, and got a swat on the head for disobeying.

"I'm not sorry for that," Sadira said. Farrin hated the sound of Sadira getting hit.

"I love you!" Farrin called out, not caring about the pain from a fresh series of blows. "I might not get to say it later, so I'm saying it now. I love you!"

"You are only making it worse for yourself," a guard said after hitting her again on the head. "You were told to be quiet. You will have plenty of chances to talk once we get to Evin. You've heard of Evin? You know who works there?"

Farrin answered, despite being told to keep silent, but her answer came out as a whisper.

"Principal Kobra?"

The guards heard her and laughed. "That's right. We're going to the principal's office. You're going to be kept after school!"

While the guards laughed, Farrin felt Sadira lean back to find her. She shifted around on the floor of the truck until their backs were pressed against each other. It was a little like hugging. Their hands, tied behind their backs, found each other, and they entwined their fingers.

They'll have to cut off my hands to get us apart, Farrin thought, even though she knew it wasn't true.

When she saw barbed wire strung along the top of a high wall, Farrin knew they were at the prison. From her vantage point on the floor of the truck, she could see no details—just wire, the wall, and the moon.

"Cover your eyes with these," one of the soldiers said, dangling pieces of cloth in front of their faces to use as blindfolds.

"You want us to tie them with our feet?" Sadira asked. "Or do you think we're magicians and can tie them with our minds?"

"I don't care what you are," the guard said, roughly binding the smelly cloths over their eyes. "You're some kind of deviant, but I don't care which kind. You won't be anything soon."

"If you're going to kill us, why cover our eyes?" Sadira asked.

Farrin squeezed her friend's fingers. *Please be quiet*, she urged silently.

Sadira didn't get the message. "If you are proud of what you are doing, if you think that what is going to happen to us is right, if you are so sure we are going to be killed, why bind our eyes?"

"I don't answer to you." Sadira cried out as she was hit again. Farrin held onto her friend's fingers as tightly as she could.

"I think it is because they are afraid of us, Farrin," Sadira said. "These men are used to getting whatever they want, and they are afraid of girls like us because we don't need them for anything!"

Farrin hated the sound that came next, of Sadira being kicked in the head. She felt Sadira's fingers slip from hers. She wiggled them, searching in the air for her friend.

The truck came to a stop.

"Get out!"

It was not easy getting out of the back of the truck blind, with their hands tied behind them. They were yanked this way, then that. Farrin had no idea which direction she was facing or where Sadira was.

"Sadira, are you here?"

"Silence!"

They were led inside and down a series of halls before reaching a small room. Their blindfolds were removed and their hands were unbound.

The first thing they did was hug each other.

The second thing they did was land hard on the floor after being struck.

"On your feet." The guards pulled them up.

They stood for a while. The room was gray and dingy, with a dim lightbulb that made the dinginess appear worse. There was a small table and a chair, and a portrait of the Ayatollah Khomeini hung on the wall.

It really is Principal Kobra's office, Farrin thought.

The door opened and a man in a green uniform came in, followed by a woman also in uniform.

"You have been arrested for deviancy," the man said, looking down at the paper the guard handed him. "This is considered a crime against society. You will be put on trial. Normally, deviants like you are given a warning, and that warning is backed up by lashes so that the message gets into your brain through your blood. I understand from our informant that you have already been given a warning, and you were ordered to desist from your deviant behavior.

Mercy has been shown to you and you have thrown it back in our faces."

"Will we be allowed to speak in our defense?" Sadira asked.

"You have a defense?" the man asked. "Give us the names of your witnesses, and we will bring them here to speak for you."

The girls were silent.

The man nodded to the woman to take them away.

The woman's grip on Farrin's arm was as hard as the male soldiers'. "Cover your eyes," she said. "And do it properly. You don't want me to catch you trying to look."

Farrin bound her eyes with the cloth. And then she panicked—she wanted one last look at Sadira in case they were separated! She tore the cloth from her eyes and saw that Sadira had done the same.

"I love you," Farrin said.

"I love you, too," said Sadira.

"I could order you both executed right now," said the man in charge. "Do you want to die? It makes no difference to me."

"I want to live," Farrin said. She smiled at Sadira and they raised their blindfolds to their eyes at the same time. They were taken from the room.

Up and down more hallways, up and down more stairs. Outside one building and into another. Some hallways smelled of bleach. Some smelled of urine. Some hallways were silent except for the sound of their own feet on the concrete. Others were full of the sounds of shouting and screaming, of begging and weeping.

Farrin couldn't tell if Sadira was still with her or not. She coughed three times. Sadira coughed back. So far, they were together.

Then Farrin's guard stopped her before a door, opened it, and shoved her inside.

"Keep your blindfold on," the guard ordered. "You don't want to be caught with it off."

The door slammed shut and was locked.

Farrin coughed three times.

No one coughed back.

Eighteen

Farrin was disobedient.

She had to know what it looked like in her cell. With her back against the door, she raised her blindfold just a bit.

The cell was a small, bare room—no beds, no toilet. The ceiling was low and the only illumination came from the hall through the narrow slot in the door, creating more shadows than light.

Still, it was enough for Farrin to see that she was not alone. Several women were sleeping on the floor at the back of the cell. Farrin was relieved. She felt safer having some company. They would be able to tell her things about the prison, and maybe they could tell her where Sadira might have been taken.

"I'm Farrin," she whispered. "Sorry to wake you. I just got here."

No one stirred.

It must be a comfort to sleep here, Farrin thought. *I will probably find comfort too, if I'm ever able to sleep again.*

She leaned against the wall and slid down to the floor. She shook from nerves and from the cold. She tried to warm up a little by wrapping her arms around herself.

Her cell was quiet, but there were other sounds all around. Not good ones. The stone walls had a strange effect on the sounds, making them seem otherworldly and nonhuman.

"Sadira is fine," she whispered to herself. "I would know if she was not fine. She's scared, of course, but she is in a cell with women who will take care of her and keep her warm. We will get through this and see each other again. My parents are mad at me, but they won't leave me in here. They have lots of money. They will bribe someone. We'll get out."

What if her parents refused to help Sadira too? "Then I will stay in here until I know Sadira is out. They know how stubborn I am. They'll have to give in."

Fresh screams rang out. Farrin clasped her hands over her ears and bit her lips so that she would not scream too.

"My parents have lots of money," she whispered again. "They won't leave me in here. How would my mother face her friends? She'd be too ashamed to have a daughter in prison. They'll get me out and I'll make them get Sadira out too. And then, even if I can't ever see Sadira again, I will be happy. Well, not happy, but I will be all right if I know Sadira is all right. And who knows? Things change. We will be adults soon. Maybe we can find a way to be together then.

"My parents will get us out. My parents will get us out. My parents will get us out."

Farrin repeated the phrase over and over, just to hear the sound of her voice.

Then she had another thought. What if her parents had been arrested? What if the Revolutionary Guard arrested the whole party for drinking alcohol and having photos of the crown prince and the Shah? If her parents were in jail, who would help her then? And if no one helped her, how would she help Sadira?

She had to have more information about the terrible place she was in. There had to be someone here who would take pity on her because she was so young, or because she had never been arrested before, or because she got good grades. There must be someone she could ask to check on her parents or to help her get a lawyer.

"Excuse me," she whispered to the sleeping women. "Excuse me. I'm sorry to wake you, but I need some help."

The women didn't stir.

Farrin raised her blindfold a little more and glance at the little door opening. No one was watching at the door. She scuttled across the floor to get closer to her cellmates.

She didn't have far to go. The cell was small. She reached out to touch the foot of one of the women and gave it a gentle shake.

"Excuse me," she said. Then, when there was no response, she shook the foot harder. "Wake up! Wake up! I need to talk to you!"

There was still no response. Farrin began to get a terrible, terrible feeling.

She had to know for sure. She inched forward until she was at the woman's head. She lifted the woman's scarf. Dead eyes stared back at her.

Farrin screamed.

And screamed. And screamed.

She slid back to the other wall and crouched, screaming. The women in the cell—they were all dead. She had been put in a cell with dead women.

The door opened suddenly behind her and she fell back against the legs of a guard.

"On your feet," the guard said. "What are you screaming for? Dead people can't hurt you. And fix your blindfold. That's the last time I'm going to tell you."

Farrin stood. Her hands were bound again, this time in front of her. Then the guard clamped her claw on Farrin's arm and pulled her down the hall.

"You are going to be asked some questions," the guard said. "It is better if you answer. Better for you, better for everyone. Would you like to tell me anything before we get to the interrogation room?"

"Where are my parents?" Farrin asked. "Have they been arrested?"

"I asked if you wanted to tell me anything, not if you wanted to ask me anything."

"My parents didn't know Sadira was in the house."

"You'll have to do better than that." They stopped before a door. "Last chance. Anything?"

Farrin didn't know how to answer. What did the guard want to know? She hesitated, trying to think, but it didn't matter. Time was up. The guard opened the door and shoved Farrin inside.

Someone pushed her down into a metal chair. She could

hear people moving around her. How many others were in the room? Someone lit a cigarette. Someone else shuffled their feet. She thought that the guard had stepped away from her but was still somewhere in the room.

Whoever was smoking dropped the cigarette to the ground when it was done and ground it out with his heel. He lit up another one. Farrin counted five cigarettes lit and dropped before the door opened and someone else entered.

Farrin's blindfold was removed.

An older man in robes instead of a military uniform sat behind the table. He silently read from a piece of paper, then he looked up at her.

"What do you have to say for yourself?" he asked. His voice was low and without inflection. It terrified Farrin more than if he had shouted.

"I have done nothing wrong," she said.

"Then why are you here?"

"Someone must have made a mistake."

"Do you think the government makes mistakes?"

Principal Kobra could work here, Farrin thought. She opened her mouth to say something back, then closed it again. She remembered Principal Kobra's words. "Be careful you do not have too much confidence."

The man looked at her as if he had all the time in the world. "What would you like to tell me about this mistake that has been made?"

"I am a good student," Farrin said. "I was second in my class last term."

"Your job is to go to school," the man said. "The people of Iran have decided to fund your education, so your job is to do well. So, you did your job. Do you want me to applaud you for doing your job?"

"No, sir."

"Do you think people applaud me when I do my job? No. That is just what is expected. Do you have anything else to say?"

"May I ask a question?"

"We are having a conversation. You do not need permission to ask questions during a conversation. Do you think I would be mad at you for asking a question?"

Farrin took a deep breath. "Where are my parents?" she asked.

"You are concerned about your parents. That is good, but that will not get you applause either. You are *supposed* to be concerned about your parents."

He hadn't answered her question.

"What else do you have to offer to me, other than your work at school and your supposed concern for your parents?"

"I don't know what you mean," Farrin said.

"Well, you could start by telling me who was the leader?"

"The leader?"

"One of you forced the other into this state of depravity. Did you force her, or did she force you?"

"No one forced anyone," Farrin said, then bit her tongue. She had been caught. She had just admitted that she was depraved.

"I won't take down that answer just yet," the man said. "I

am merciful, and you might want to change your mind later. Who else was involved in your depravity?"

Farrin did not reply.

"The Head Girl at your school, the girl named Rabia—was she the one who recruited you to this way of life?"

Farrin was startled to hear Rabia's name.

"Rabia? How is she? Is she here?"

"She was."

There was something about the way he said it that held Farrin back from asking more.

He stopped talking then, and they just sat.

After a number of minutes had ticked by, he spoke again.

"Are you prepared to give us the names of the others involved in your activities?"

"What activities?" Farrin asked. She was now genuinely confused. Did he mean her mother's Bring Back the Shah meetings? Did he mean writing stories about demon hunters? What did he mean?

He clarified it for her.

"It is clear that you have engaged in illegal, immoral activities with the girl named Sadira. This is a growing problem in Iran. Young women and young men in Iran think they can do whatever they want. They are mimicking the indecency of the West, and we mean to bring it to a stop. It is against God and it is against nature. What you have done is treason against the established order. The only way you might save yourself is if you tell us who else is involved in this. Give us names if you hope to save yourself."

Who else? Were there other girls who felt the way Farrin and Sadira felt? In spite of hrself, Farrin smiled. She was glad that there were other girls who felt as happy as she had felt. She was not alone.

"You seem to take this situation lightly," the man said. "That is an interesting response. Do you have anything more to say to me?"

"Let us go," Farrin said.

The man motioned to Farrin's guard. The blindfold went back on Farrin's face and she was taken from the room.

"Where are you taking me?" she asked. "Don't put me back in that cell! Don't put me back in that cell with the dead people. Don't put me back there!"

She dropped to the floor. She would not help them! She would not move one inch if they were taking her back to that awful room!

"You won't be going back to that room," the guard said. "At least, not while you're breathing."

Other arms pulled her up and dragged her down the hall.

They took her to another corridor and pushed her to the wall.

"Sit," they said.

She sat.

Nineteen

Her blindfold was tight, so she could not see, but she could hear other people around her.

No one was talking, but they still made sounds. Farrin listened hard and was able to tell that others were sitting nearby in a row along the wall, to the left of her. Guards walked back and forth along the line of prisoners. Farrin could tell they were guards because of the sound of their army boots against the concrete floor. She wanted to say Sadira's name but did not. Sadira would have responded, and then both of them would be beaten.

Then she remembered their signal.

She coughed three times.

There was no reply.

Time passed. Farrin had no way to keep track of it. If daylight could penetrate the corridor, she couldn't see it through her blindfold. Could daylight penetrate hell?

Every now and then, someone called out a name and Farrin heard the sounds of a prisoner getting to their feet and then being guided into another room.

Sometimes she could hear shouting. She was able to decipher some of the words. "Give us a name!" "Tell us what you know!" The questions were often followed by screams. Sometimes the screams went on and on.

Shut up! Farrin wanted to yell. The sounds were unbearable. More screams, the crack of a lash hitting human skin, the sound of bone hitting bone. Sounds that Farrin could not begin to identify.

I'm in an Edgar Allen Poe story, she thought. I am in "The Pit and the Pendulum."

Her back hurt from tension and from sitting on the floor. Her legs cramped up and the blindfold was so tight that it was making her head ache. She tried to loosen the blindfold by rubbing the side of her face against her shoulder. Bit by bit, the blindfold shifted slightly. She kept working at it, stopping whenever she heard the boots of the Revolutionary Guard nearby.

She worked slowly, so that no one would notice what she was doing. Prisoners came and went from the line. Sometimes a door would open and she heard a sound like dragging across the floor, then that noise would stop and be replaced by other sounds. When the screaming stopped, she could hear people whispering prayers. The stench was terrible. People were urinating and defecating on themselves, and everywhere there was a smell of sweat and fear mixed with stale tobacco and blood.

She kept nudging her blindfold until all it once it fell away.

"Blindfold on!"

The guard stood at the other end of the line. Farrin had just moments to look around her. She did not dwell on the bodies and wounded people lying nearby. She had to know if Sadira or her parents were there. To her left she saw a long line of prisoners that reached to the wall where the hallway ended. To her right, the hallway went on forever. So did the line of prisoners. She looked as far as she could before the guard reached her and pointed his rifle at her head.

"Blindfold on!"

There was just enough give in the rope that bound her hands for her to get the blindfold cloth around her head. It was awkward to tie—her headscarf was in the way, and when that slipped, her hair got tangled up in the blindfold. Farrin's hands shook. The guard's rifle was still inches from her face.

"Keep it on!"

Where was Sadira? Where were her parents? Maybe Sadira was already out. They'd know that Farrin would refuse to leave without her friend, so they got Sadira out first. The calmed Farrin. She took her mind out of the blood and fear and sent it back to the gymnasium, where she and Sadira studied.

She managed to fall asleep.

Cough, cough, cough.

Sadira was in her dream, reaching out to her, tucking a strand of hair into her headscarf.

Cough, cough, cough.

Why are you coughing, Sadira? Farrin thought in her dream. *I'm right here. You can just talk to me.*

Then she sat bolt upright.

Had someone really coughed three times?

She coughed three times too, hoping for an answer.

There was nothing, just the endless weeping and praying in the hallway, along with screaming from one of the rooms.

She tried again, then held her breath to listen.

"Farrin Kazemi." A guardswoman called her name.

"I'm here!" she shouted. "My name is Farrin Kazemi. I'm here and I'm all right!"

Before she could hear if there was a response from Sadira or her parents, the guard pulled her to her feet and dragged her into a room. Then he tore off her blindfold.

She was in another small room with another robed man who sat behind another desk.

"You will please sign this confession," the man said. He pushed a piece of paper toward her.

"What confession?" Farrin asked. "I have not confessed to anything. I am not signing anything. I want to see my parents."

"I will tell you again. You will please pick up the pen and sign this confession."

They can't make me sign if I don't want to. If I don't sign anything, they can't hold me for anything.

"I'm not signing."

The man in the robe nodded at the guard, who blindfolded her again and hustled her out of the office.

They turned to the right and started down the long hallway of prisoners. The blindfold had been reapplied a little high, so Farrin could just make out some of the faces of the people on the floor.

"I'm Farrin," she whispered over and over, until she got a swat in the head to shut her up.

The guard took her outside. They walked for a long time. Farrin stumbled more than once over rocks or steps or something else—she couldn't tell.

At last they stopped. The guardswoman removed Farrin's blindfold.

They were in front of a gallows. Six people swung from ropes along the crossbeam. A line of blindfolded prisoners stood near the platform steps, waiting to be hung.

"This really is your last chance," the guard said. "You are young, so we are being merciful. But this is it. We have too much to do right now. We don't have time to play around with a little deviant who won't confess her transgressions."

Farrin looked around wildly. She still couldn't see Sadira or her parents. The guard left the blindfold off as she took Farrin over to the lineup of prisoners awaiting execution.

"Shooting is faster," said the guard. "We've done a lot of that. We'll probably have to go back to it—hanging is so slow. But sometimes there are advantages in taking the extra time. Sometimes it can be good to give someone a chance to think things over."

Around her, Farrin heard more prayers and weeping.

"Do you want me to leave you in this line?" the guard asked. "I hear you are good at your studies. Here is a bit of math for you. We hang six people at one time. Each group hanging takes around twenty minutes. There are thirty people in this line in front of you. If I leave you here, how much time do you have left to live?"

Farrin began to cry. The sky was blue and the sun was bright, and she knew that beyond the wall of the prison people lived their lives, went to school, tried to be happy. She prayed that Sadira was among them.

If there is any chance at all that she is out there, then I want to live, Farrin decided.

"I'll sign the confession," she said.

"What? I can't hear you."

"I'll sign the confession."

"Are you sure? I don't want to take you all the way back to the office only to bring you back out here. That would not put me in a very good mood."

"I'll sign it," Farrin said. "I will. I promise. I want to."

The guard shrugged. "If that's what you want. It's up to you."

Farrin was ready to go back, but now the guard didn't seem to be in a hurry at all. She left Farrin in line and started chatting with another guard. More blindfolded prisoners were pushed into the line behind her. As the executions went on, Farrin shuffled closer and closer to the scaffold steps.

"Do you know where you are?" Farrin asked the man behind her. "They're going to hang you. They're going to hang everybody."

"They have already hung my whole family," said the man. "At least, what was left of it after the war. I don't want to be here. I want to join them. They're not killing me. They are sending me back to the people I love."

"But if we all fight back—"

"Shhh," the man said. "I have no fight left. Now, I just want to pray and think of my family. Allow me this small bit of peace."

"God be with you," Farrin said.

"And with you," the man replied.

Six more bodies were taken down. The line moved forward again.

This is close enough, she decided. She left the line and approached her guard. "I'm still here," she said.

The two guards looked at her then at each other.

"Is this the deviant?" the other guard asked.

"Yup. This is it."

"I hope it isn't catching."

The guardswoman took her arm and marched her back to the office. The robed man put the confession in front of Farrin. She started to read it.

"Don't waste our time!"

She signed her name at the bottom.

The man took up the piece of paper and looked at Farrin's signature. He stood up.

"Farrin Kazemi, you have confessed to acts of homosexuality and deviancy, in violation of the laws and morals of the state, and are hereby declared an enemy of the people. You are sentenced to hanging until you are dead. That is all."

"What?" Farrin cried. "But I thought if I signed I would avoid death! What is this? I want the confession back! You can't do this! I'm only fifteen!"

"Before you signed the confession, you were going to be hanged for noncooperation," the man said. "Now that you have confessed, you will be hung for your crime. That is all."

Farrin shouted her objections all the way down the hallways as she was hauled off and thrown into another cell. The door slammed behind her.

She was alone.

At least this time there were no dead bodies in there with her.

Twenty

"You have a visitor."

The guard gave Farrin a gentle nudge with her foot to wake her up.

"A visitor?"

"On your feet. Unless you don't want to see anyone."

Farrin stood up. "Who is visiting me? Is it one of my parents? Which one?" Strangely, she hoped the visitor was her mother. Her father had been kinder to her all her life, but her mother was fierce. If anyone could get her out, it would be her mother.

Naturally there was no answer.

The guard took her to a room with a few tables and chairs. Farrin looked around for her parents. They were not there.

The only person in the room was a woman in a black chador. Her back was to the door. Then she turned around.

It was Principal Kobra.

Farrin blinked several times, trying to understand what she saw.

Farrin sat down uneasily across from her principal. It seemed as if years had passed since she was a student.

"How are you?" Principal Kobra asked.

"I can't believe you're here."

"Why can't you believe it?" Principal Kobra asked. "I'll tell you why. Because you have a closed mind. You put people into a certain category and then you never bother to investigate whether or not you have made a mistake."

Farrin was confused. Had her principal come all this way just to lecture her? Did it mean that much to her to make Farrin feel worse?

"How are you?" the principal asked again.

"I'm scared."

"I suppose you are."

Principal Kobra seemed uncomfortable. *You should be*, Farrin thought. *You are old and you are going to walk out of here and live your life. I am young and I will die horribly—all because of that government you are so fond of.* But she said none of that. There seemed no point to arguing anymore.

"Is there any news of my parents?" she asked instead, not really expecting there would be.

"Your parents have left the country," Principal Kobra said. "They bribed the guards and left without answering for their crimes."

"They left me behind?"

"It would seem so."

"What about—what about Sadira?"

"Sadira is also here."

"Will you be able to see her?"

"I don't know," said Principal Kobra. She seemed bewildered. "It was harder than I thought it would be to get permission to see you. Things here seem…chaotic."

Farrin had no sympathy for the woman. "What did you expect it to be like?"

Principal Kobra shook her head. "There is that closed mind again. You see me as cold and severe, and that's all you see. Unfortunately, you are not the first student I have visited here."

"Do you want me to thank you? Do you know that they are going to kill us?"

Principal Kobra slowly nodded.

"Can you help us?" Farrin asked. "Can you keep them from hanging us?"

Principal Kobra looked into Farrin's eyes. "I have never lied to a student and I will not lie to you now. You must accept your fate. I came to tell you that you have a good mind and a good heart. In spite of everything, I am glad you were a student at my school. I came to tell you this, and to give you what comfort I could."

Principal Kobra lifted a bag and placed it on the table.

"I brought you a blanket," she said, opening the bag. "The guards said I could give it to you. I know those cells are cold."

Farrin was about to thank her and reach for the blanket when she suddenly had a thought. She looked under the table. There was no other bag.

Principal Kobra had brought only one blanket.

"Give it to Sadira," Farrin said.

"Farrin, I don't know if I will be able to see Sadira. It was hard enough to see you."

"I can't be warm if I think she's cold!" Farrin exclaimed, her eyes filling with tears. "How could you think I would be warm if Sadira is cold?"

"Farrin—"

"I love her," Farrin sobbed. "You don't understand! We just want to be together. We don't want to die!"

She put her head on her arms and wept.

Principal Kobra put a hand on Farrin's head.

"I am one hundred percent behind the revolution," she said. "I was there at the beginning of it and I will defend it all my life. But in my revolution, we do not execute children. I am sorry that this is happening to you."

Farrin raised her head and wiped her tears on her sleeves. She pushed the blanket across the table.

"While you are defending the revolution," she said, "take this blanket to Sadira."

And then the guard stepped forward. Their time was up.

Principal Kobra embraced Farrin.

Farrin clung to the woman. It didn't matter that she was still angry with her old principal. Farrin needed to be hugged, and there was no one else.

"I will get the blanket to Sadira," the principal said. "I will tell her that it is from you, and that you want her to be warm."

"Thank you," whispered Farrin.

Principal Kobra tightened her embrace. "Rest easy, my child. When the hard part comes, think of the poems that have given you the greatest joy. Think of happy times and of those you love. Carry those good thoughts with you as you leave this world."

"If you can get word to my parents, will you tell them that I'm sorry?"

Principal Kobra looked into Farrin's eyes. "Are you?"

Farrin thought of Sadira and how precious their time had been. "No," she admitted.

"That's my good student," Principal Kobra whispered to her. "Truth is always the most important thing, even when it leads us into dark places."

The guard pulled Farrin away and took her back to her cell.

She did not know how much time she had left. She wrapped her arms around herself and thought about Sadira —wrapped in the blanket and feeling warm and loved.

For two more days she kept the vision in her head as she shivered in her cell.

On the third day, a guard came for her.

It was time to die.

Twenty-One

"Will someone come to claim your body?" the guard said.

"What?"

"Your body. What are we supposed to do with your body after we take it down from the scaffold?"

Farrin had not eaten since her arrest. She was exhausted, chilled to the bone and so terrified of what was about to happen that she could not think. She had no answer for the guard.

"Another one for the field, then," the guard said. "As long as I don't have to be the one digging. Sometimes we make the prisoners dig their own graves, but they dawdle and take all day. Fine with me when the weather is good. But we're just so backed up. These days, get a bit off schedule and you're working around the clock just to get caught up. What about a shroud?"

"What?"

It was as much as Farrin could get out.

"Don't tell me you don't have a shroud, either? Your family is going to be charged for that if we have to provide one. I don't know how the front office staff spends their time. They certainly don't spend it taking care of the most basic details. Well, we can worry about the shroud later. First, let's get you hung."

Farrin stumbled along beside her guard as the woman chatted casually.

"A lot of people, when they get to this stage, are actually happy to have it all over," the guard said. "I think the worrying and the waiting must be terrible. Sometimes people are arrested and they are executed within the hour. Better to be kind like that, I figure. Other guards disagree with me. They say that when citizens are made to suffer, they learn obedience. It makes them better members of society. But if we are going to kill them anyway, what is the point of all that extra suffering? It certainly messes up the floors, let me tell you!"

The guard sounded as if what was about to happen was nothing out of the ordinary. Farrin realized that, to the guard, it *was* a routine. Just a regular day for her.

Get up, put on your uniform, have breakfast, go to work, escort women to their death, go home, have supper, go to bed.

"Guard, would you come over here for a second?" Farrin heard someone call.

"I'm on my way to make a delivery," the guard said.

"Let someone else do it. There are forms you need to fill out in order to receive your pay."

"I filled those out already."

"Well, apparently you didn't do them right, because you have to fill them out again. Just come and do it now, okay? Then I can get my filing done."

"All right." She propped Farrin up against a wall. "Stay here."

Farrin's hands were bound and her blindfold was tight. If she took a few steps she would probably fall. *It could be worth it, though,* she thought. *I might get away.*

She was about to try when someone else took her elbow.

"I'll take the prisoner up," a male guard said. "After you finish the forms, why not take your break?"

"Fine with me," the woman guard said.

Farrin walked alongside the male guard. She was relieved to get away from the woman's inane chatter. If this was going to be the last few moments of her life, she wanted a little peace. She wanted to think about Sadira. She wanted to remember being happy.

"Do not react in any way," the guard said quietly. "I have been hired by your father to get you out, but you must do exactly as I say, when I say it. Do you understand?"

Farrin's heart jumped. Her parents had not abandoned her!

"What about Sadira?" she asked.

"Already taken care of," the guard told her. "Your father said you would refuse to leave without her, so we got her out yesterday. But they are on the alert today, so this will be difficult. Quiet now. People are approaching."

Farrin listened intently, waiting for a signal to come. The guard exchanged pleasantries with some other guards. Gunshots sounded a little ways off.

"That's just the firing squad," the guard said as he pulled her along again. "Get ready."

He changed direction abruptly, walking very fast. Farrin kept pace beside him. Suddenly she was lifted off the ground and into the back of a truck. She was buried under a mound of stinking clothes.

She felt the truck start up. She could feel it drive forward, stop, start again, stop, start again, then turn and pick up speed.

We're on the highway, she thought. *We're out of Evin Prison.*

The truck had turned left instead of right. They were going north, away from Tehran.

We're heading into the mountains, Farrin thought. *We're heading for the sea.*

She stayed quiet and still as the drive went on. She didn't care about the cramps in her shoulders or the stink that surrounded her. Whatever was ahead was infinitely better than what lay behind.

A long time passed. The truck stopped once to refuel, then they were back on the road. It wasn't until nightfall that the driver pulled off the highway and came to a stop.

Farrin heard him get out of the cab of the truck and come around to the back.

"Farrin? Are you all right?"

The stinking clothes were pulled away. Farrin looked up. It was Ahmad.

"Your father bribed some of the guards," he said. "We're going to get you out of Iran. Your parents have already left the country."

"What about Sadira?"

"We got Sadira out first," Ahmad said. "She will be waiting for you when we cross the border." He helped her sit up and gave her water and some food.

"We need to keep moving. Are you okay back here for a while longer?"

Of course she was. Farrin crawled back under the pile of clothes and Ahmad started driving again. She wiggled around in the pile so that she was able to clear some more space around her face. The night air was cool and fresh.

She was stunned. One minute she was about to die, and the next minute she had a chance to live. To be with Sadira! The back of the truck was all closed up and Farrin was in total darkness, but she knew that she was moving away from death and toward freedom.

The road was bumpy. Ahmad was probably staying off the main highways in hopes of avoiding the checkpoints.

Farrin couldn't see it, but she knew the moon was out there. She knew that Sadira was somewhere safe, under their moon, waiting for her.

I can't wait, Farrin thought. *I can't wait to see her. Oh, I was so wrong about my parents! When I see them again I will apologize and completely mean it. Even though Sadira will be by my side, I will be the sort of daughter they can be proud of. I will do anything they ask—even join their Bring Back the Shah campaign if they want me to!*

Although the road was rough, the pile of clothes cushioned her. Farrin told herself she was too excited to sleep—she needed to stay awake so she would be ready for whatever was next. But she was exhausted, and the truck's rocking motion finally sent her to sleep. For the rest of the night and into the next morning, Farrin slept deeply, without dreams.

Twenty-Two

Farrin was startled awake by a sudden flood of light. Someone had opened the back of the truck.

She had the presence of mind to hold still. Her face was hidden enough, she hoped. If someone was doing a quick inspection, they might not notice she was there.

"We need to change cars," Ahmad said. "You must get up. Be quick."

Farrin was quick. On wobbly legs she got down from the truck.

"Put this on," Ahmad instructed her, handing her a blue Afghan burqa. It was different from the black Iranian chador. The chador still allowed a woman's face to show. The burqa was like a tent, covering everything, including her face. A small cloth screen across her eyes was just open enough to see through.

It was a full, awkward garment and she had never worn anything like it. She struggled to figure out how to put it on.

"Hurry!" Ahmad said. "Put it on!"

Instinctively, she was about to remind him that he was a servant and she was the boss's daughter, but instead she thought better of it and held her tongue. She managed to get the burqa on and followed Ahmad to a small car parked beside the truck.

"Whose car is this?" she asked.

"This is all part of the arrangement made by your father," Ahmad said. "It is good to change cars, in case we are being followed. And now we have a full tank of gas. We need to keep driving."

"Can I take this off while we are in the car?"

"Leave it on."

Farrin left it. What did it matter? They were heading down a highway again, moving ever closer to Sadira. Farrin did not care what she wore. The burqa made a good disguise. As long as no one looked under it, she could be anybody.

If she rewrote her demon-hunting story again, maybe the hunters should wear burqas. She wasn't sure if there had ever been a burqa-wearing woman solving mysteries in a story before.

On the seat next to her were bread and a bottle of warm orange soda. It was a bit of a challenge to eat while wearing the awkward garment, but Farrin managed.

"Where are we?" she asked. "I thought we were heading to the Caspian Sea."

"We are going to Pakistan," Ahmad said. "That is the best way. It is too dangerous to go through Turkey. The border is more open in Pakistan. By that, I mean that there are more places to cross into Pakistan that are not properly protected by border guards."

"Is that where Sadira is waiting?"

"You have no reason to worry about Sadira," Ahmad said. "Sadira is safe now. Now, be quiet. We are coming to a checkpoint."

Revolutionary Guards had set up a checkpoint across the highway. Through the screen over her eyes, Farrin could see men and women with guns, stopping cars and examining identification papers.

"You will let me talk, and if they ask you questions, you will agree with whatever I say," Ahmad said. "Keep your eyes on the floor of the car. Do not look up. They will wonder why you are so curious. Do you understand?"

"Yes," said Farrin.

It was their turn. Ahmad rolled down the window and presented his papers.

Farrin kept her eyes on the floor. She heard the guard fan out the papers as he looked them over.

"Afghan?" the guard said.

"Yes," said Ahmad.

"Papers for her?"

"She is my wife," said Ahmad. He reached in front of Farrin and into the glove compartment of the car. She could see his hand take out something. "Here is our marriage paper."

The guard took his time looking at it. "What are you doing on the road?"

"I was in Mashhad. I heard that someone was hiring Afghans for construction. But when I arrived, all the jobs had been taken."

The guard considered this a little longer, then he handed back the papers and waved them along.

Farrin waited until they were well away from the checkpoint before she asked, "Where did you get those papers?"

"Your father knows the right people," he replied. "I don't know who they are. They make up certificates."

"So it's all fake, then."

"I am just your father's servant," Ahmad said.

They kept driving. Farrin asked about Sadira a few more times, but Ahmad had nothing more to say. She struggled to stay awake. The heat in the car and the lack of fresh air under the burqa made it difficult to remain alert. In spite of her best efforts, she dozed off more than once. Each time she surfaced, she came to with a start.

The sun was setting when they pulled into a refugee camp. Ahmad got out of the car and left her sitting there while he went off to talk to the men in the camp. Farrin felt conspicuous sitting in the car by herself. Anyone who passed by looked through the window at her. She told herself that they couldn't see her face, that all they saw was a woman in a burqa, but she still felt vulnerable. She could no longer see Ahmad. What if someone asked her what she was doing there? What would she tell them? That her husband had gone off and left her? Wouldn't they know she was a stranger?

Finally, after a long time, Ahmad returned. "Get out," he said, opening her door.

"Where have you been?" she asked.

"Don't speak," he said.

A thousand comebacks popped into her head, but she forced herself to keep mute.

Just get me to Sadira, she said to him in her mind. *Get me to Sadira.*

He led her through the assortment of tents, rag shelters, and lean-tos made of trash to a tent on the far side of the camp.

"You'll sleep here," he said to her.

Then he left.

Here was a tent already crowded with women and children. But it wasn't fun like it had been at her grandparents' place. There were not enough blankets. Some of the younger children coughed all night—deep chest coughs that sounded nothing like a regular cold. She wasn't sure if it was all right for her to take her burqa off, so she left it on all night. Several times she woke up in the night struggling for breath, as the burqa had tightened itself around her as she slept.

The next day, not knowing what else to do, Farrin sat inside the tent and did not talk to anyone. Some of the women asked her questions, but she pretended not to understand. After a few times, they left her alone. They had enough other things to worry about.

Ahmad collected her at last, and she followed along behind him as they headed out of the camp.

He led her to another vehicle, this time a small pickup truck with a cover over the back. He gestured for her to ride in the back while he sat up front with the driver. It was crowded in the back, full of women and children and sheep and chickens, but she climbed on. The other women squeezed over to make room for her. She had her choice between holding a small child or a cage full of live chickens on her lap. When she hesitated, someone handed her the chickens. She gripped the bars of the cage to keep it from falling. Chickens pecked at her fingers.

She had no idea how long she would have to sit like this. Her body cramped up from sitting in the same position for so long. She wanted to talk to Ahmad but did not want to draw attention to herself. So she sat and endured the pain. Every uncomfortable kilometer brought her closer to Sadira.

Hours later, the truck pulled over to the side of the road. Ahmad appeared at the back.

"Out," he said.

There were several women in burqas in the back, so Ahmad didn't know which one he was talking to, but Farrin knew. She passed the chickens on to someone else and staggered out of the truck. Her feet were asleep. She stamped them and looked around.

All she could see was a whole lot of nothing.

"From here, we walk," Ahmad said. He handed her a small bundle. "There is a bottle of water in here, and some food. It is a long journey, so don't waste them."

Farrin didn't know how long they walked over the bare, rocky hills, which were hot as an oven during the day and bone-chilling at night.

"The border is just ahead," said Ahmad. "We must be

extremely careful here. We need to avoid the Iranian and Pakistani guards. And there are bandits who rob the refugees. Stay close and do what I tell you."

Farrin did. When Ahmad said to go flat, she threw herself onto the ground and kept her head down. When Ahmad said to run, she ran, ignoring the angry blisters that now covered her feet. They scrambled up hills and down valleys, dodging behind boulders and tripping on rocks.

"Get in here," Ahmad said, pointing to a crevice in the rocks. "We will wait until nightfall and cross over into Pakistan once it is dark. Don't move. I will be back."

Farrin squeezed herself into a small space between the rocks. All she could see from there was the blue sky and the tops of distant rocky hills. It was a new kind of torture to stay put and to stay quiet, especially when she heard cars drive by. She could not see where she was and she had no way to escape if someone found her. All she could do was watch the sky turn from blue to gray to black.

The night was well underway, and Farrin was ready to jump out of her hole and take her own chances when Ahmad appeared again.

"Come. Quickly," he ordered.

I can't wait to get away from him, she thought, scrambling after Ahmad on legs that had, once again, gone to sleep.

She stayed behind him and pulled her burqa close to her face—it was the only way she could see anything through the screen. It was difficult to breathe. She had to keep choosing between breathing and seeing.

The walk seemed to go on for hours. Finally, just below the crest of a hill, Ahmad stopped.

"We're here," he said. "We're in Pakistan. We are out of Iran."

TWENTY-THREE

Farrin wanted to toss off her burqa and do a celebration dance. But before she could move a muscle, Ahmad stopped her.

"Keep covered," he said. "Follow me."

Your days of ordering me around are numbered, Farrin thought but did as she was told. They climbed up the rest of the hill. At the top, Farrin paused. Below them stretched a huge refugee camp. She saw tents and mud houses—and lots and lots of people.

"What is this?" she asked.

Ahmad did not answer.

"Are my parents here?"

He just walked faster.

She had no choice but to follow after him.

They entered the camp. She stayed close behind him as he hurried through the winding alleys and narrow walkways. The stench was terrible. On either side of them ran an open sewer.

Flies, children, and garbage were everywhere. A man approached them pushing a cart piled high with oranges. He kept coming even though the pathway was too narrow. Farrin struggled to keep her balance, but she tottered and stepped off. One of her feet landed right in the stream of sewage.

"Look what you've done!" Ahmad scolded her. "How will you get clean? This is not good!"

He kept walking. He didn't even offer to help her out of the stream.

She tried to step back onto the path, but her feet kept slipping. Finally another woman in a burqa took pity on her, held out her arm, and helped Farrin back on the path.

Farrin thanked her and hurried after Ahmad.

Finally he stopped in front of a gate set into a high mud wall. The opening had a torn, dirty curtain over it. He pulled it aside and called in.

People came forward and greeted him. They led him to a seat and brought him tea. Then they gathered around and talked. Farrin stood by the entrance and waited. She was afraid to reveal her face in case it was the wrong thing to do.

They all spoke in a language Farrin didn't recognize. She was surprised to hear Ahmad converse so easily. He had always spoken Farsi with her. At one point it was clear they were talking about her, as he pointed at the filth on her foot and everyone turned to stare.

Finally, several women came over to her and took her away to another part of the little compound. She could see that there were a few mud houses and lean-tos enclosed by the wall. It was a relief when they took off her burqa and the fresh air cooled her face and entered her lungs.

"Are my parents here?" she asked, but the women did not appear to understand her. They helped clean her up and then left her alone.

Farrin sat and waited. A large group of children stopped in front of her and gawked at her as if she were some sort of entertainment. They all had runny noses and matted hair. Their clothes were filthy and most were barefoot.

"Hello," she said. The children just giggled.

Someone brought her a cup of tea and some bread. She started to eat—she was starving! But the children's eyes widened as they watched her. At last she held out the bread to them. They grabbed it and devoured it within seconds.

Work went on all around her. The women carried in buckets of water and attempted to bathe the children and wash some clothes. A girl about her age swept the dirt in the yard with a broom made of a few branches tied together. Bedding was spread out to air in the sun. Other women brought in a bucket full of animal dung, patted it into flat pancakes and slapped them onto the wall of one of the huts. Farrin could not figure out why they were doing that until one woman broke up some of the dried dung pancakes and used them to fuel a cook fire.

It was interesting for a little while, but finally she became impatient and went looking for Ahmad. She found him in one of the huts, drinking tea and talking with some men.

"Where are my parents?" she asked. "Where is Sadira?"

Ahmad jerked his head, indicating that she should leave the hut.

"Where are my parents?" she said again. "You said Sadira would be waiting for me. Can we go there now? Why are we spending so much time here?"

"You should not interrupt us," Ahmad said. "Right now, we are talking."

"Talk away," Farrin said. "I don't care. But let me know what is going on. How long are we going to be here?"

Ahmad stood up angrily and pushed her out into the yard.

"You cannot talk to me like that anymore," he said. "I am no longer someone you can boss around and threaten."

"All right," Farrin agreed. "Fair enough. I understand. You have done your last job for my father and you don't work for him anymore. I just want to know what is going on. That's all. How long do we stay here? When will I see Sadira?"

"We are staying."

She waited a moment for Ahmad to say more. He didn't.

"We are staying? Where? For how long?"

"As long as I say," he said. He took a paper out of his pocket and unfolded it. Even before he was finished, Farrin knew what it was. Her heart sank.

"This paper says we are married," Ahmad said. "This is part of my payment for saving your life. Your father gave me money and he gave me you. The paper is real. You are my wife."

With that, he refolded the paper and turned to go back to the other men.

"I never consented to this," Farrin said. "I don't want to

be married to anybody, and certainly not to you."

"You are alive," Ahmad said. "You should thank me, but it doesn't matter. This is your home now. We are staying here. You are not going to be waited on in a big fancy house anymore. You will have to work. The other women will teach you what to do, and you had better do it and not make me look bad, as if I can't control my wife."

"What about Sadira?" Farrin asked.

"You should be grateful to your parents," he said. "You spat on their family honor; they had no need to spare you. But they paid a lot of money to save your life and to save you from yourself."

"Sadira," Farrin said again. And then she knew what he was going to say.

"That was part of the arrangement," Ahmad said. "Your father wanted you out of prison, and he wanted to put an end to your deviance."

"What happened?" Farrin asked, even though she dreaded to hear it.

"She was hung," Ahmad said. "Sadira is dead."

TWENTY-FOUR

The demon hunter's heart was broken.

Her love, her heart, her joy was dead—killed by demons who exist only to celebrate death. They take the shape of leaders on the world stage, posing for cameras and lying to their people, receiving flowers from small children at public events and then killing others in the darkness of prisons and in the white light of bombs.

The demon hunter does not know how she will go on without the companion who gave her a reason to live. They had only a brief time together and still there are so many more demons to fight.

The demon hunter is on the edge of surrender, on the edge of submission—that mortal act of bowing down, of allowing injustice to kill the fighting spirit in all creatures. It would be a relief, she thinks, to forget everything she knows about standing up and speaking out. It would be so much easier to forget everything she knows to be true.

She looks at those around her. They mean well. They work hard and struggle against terrible odds just to stay alive one more day. There is nothing undignified about them, only about what the world has done to them. Joining them in their daily toil would not be a curse, since work itself is never a curse, and poverty is an injustice, not a decree from God.

But it would not be her truth. If she submits, the demon hunter knows that a large part of her will die. She will become a shell, empty of all but grief, but soon to be filled with bitterness and rage.

The demon hunter watches the day change into evening, and the evening change into night. She sits and watches and thinks and waits.

And when the full moon rises over the wall and shines down on her, she gets to her feet. She slips into shadow and passes through the gate.

She puts one foot in front of the other, and the moon stays with her.

She doesn't know where she is going. She doesn't know when the next demons will appear.

But she will keep on walking.

She will follow the moon.

Author's Note

At the beginning of the summer of 2013, I met a woman who told me about her early years in Iran—a story that eventually became this book. She wanted to share her experience, but she needed to keep her identity secret to protect the members of her family who are still in Iran. Some of the details have been changed, but this story is essentially hers.

Iran is a great nation of poets and scientists, of filmmakers and craftspeople, of athletes and academics. It is a land of many cultures and points of view, full of people who are reaching out to engage the rest of the world. It is also a nation of deeply held traditional and religious beliefs, full of people whose vision does not embrace coexistence and progress. And, like every nation, its history is full of the push-pull between these two ways of thinking.

Iran has been inhabited for over 10,000 years. Since 1501, the beginning of the Safavid Dynasty, until the revolution in

1979, Iran was ruled by a Shah or king. The early twentieth century saw a demand from the people to have more say in the running of their country. A parliament was created in 1906, but its powers were limited.

In 1908 the British petroleum companies discovered oil in Iran. During World War I, Iran was occupied by the British, the Ottomans, and the Russians, who all wanted to secure their grasp on the oil supply lines.

A military coup in 1921 put Reza Khan Pahlavi in power as the new Shah. He pushed for modernization—roads, telephones, radio, cinema, schools—but did so at the expense of human rights and their religious traditions. He also became friendly with the Nazi regime. In 1941, Soviet and British forces, who were back in Iran protecting the oil supply, ousted the Shah. In his place, they enthroned his son, Mohammad Reza Pahlavi, who remained Shah for almost thirty-eight years.

The new Shah was very young when he took power. The parliament used the opportunity to gain strength and hold popular elections. In 1951, the prime minister, Mohammad Mosaddeq, moved to nationalize the Iranian oil industry, taking it out of foreign hands to keep the profits in Iran. He was kicked out of power later that year in a coup orchestrated by the American CIA and the British MI6.

From then on, the Shah held onto power with the military support of the United States. The Shah's secret police—known as SAVAK—arrested, tortured, and executed political opponents. In 1964, the country's spiritual leader, Ayatollah Ruhollah Khomeini, was sent into exile.

Opposition to the Shah, and to his backers in the West, grew until in the 1979 Revolution, when the Shah was forced to leave the country. Ayatollah Khomeini returned from exile and became the Supreme Leader of Iran.

Not long after the revolution, Iraq, backed with weapons supplied by the United States, attacked Iran. The war between the countries lasted ten years. Iraq used chemical weapons, and it is estimated that 100,000 Iranians died in the attacks. The Ayatollah Khomeini declared chemical weapons to be against God, and the country never used them against Iraq. Instead, Iran sent waves of soldiers across the front lines, many of them children. In 1988, by the end of the war, up to one million Iranians had died.

In the months after the war, the Iranian government stepped up its battle against those Iranians it considered to be enemies of the state. Thousands were executed.

According to the Iranian gay human rights group Homan, over 4,000 lesbian and gay Iranians have been executed since 1979.

Iran is not the only nation that still imposes a death sentence on lesbians and gays. Others, as of the end of 2013, are Saudi Arabia, Mauritania, the Republic of Sudan, Yemen, and parts of Nigeria and Somalia. In more than seventy countries spread over Asia, Africa, the Americas, Europe, and the Caribbean, being gay or lesbian is a criminal act. Some countries impose fines. Others sentence lesbians and gays to hard labor or time in prison. In Barbados and Sierra Leone, gays and lesbians can be sentenced to life in prison. In Dominica, they are forced into psychiatric "treatment," and in Malaysia, they can be whipped.

For more information about gay rights in Iran and around the world, check out:

Amnesty International at: www.amnesty.org

The International Gay and Lesbian Human Rights Organization at: www.iglhrc.org

The Gay and Lesbian Arab Society at: www.glas.org

The Iranian Railroad for Queer Refugees at: www.english.irqr.net

The Iranian gay human rights group Homan at: www.homan.se/English.htm

As a proud, gay woman, I am honored to have been entrusted with the story of Farrin and Sadira, and I hope that the real-life Farrin will be able to spend the rest of her life with whatever peace and happiness she is able to find.

Deborah Ellis, 2014

Acknowledgements

I would like to acknowledge and thank Ann Featherstone and Gail Winskill for all their hard work in helping to shape this book. I am deeply appreciative of the real-life Farrin for trusting me with her story. Thanks also to my father, Keith Ellis, and to Heidy Van Dyk for their ongoing encouragement. And I owe so much to the women and men who went before me, who stood up for their truth, took the blows, suffered the hatred and loneliness, and paved the way for me to live a much, much easier life.

Moon at Nine
Book Club Guide

Farrin describes her life as full of secrets. But she is not the only character with something to hide. Discuss the secrets kept by the other characters in this story and how those secrets reflect their vision of the world. Is there anyone who does not have a secret?

Why do you think that Farrin has chosen a demon hunter as her alter ego? Sadira asks her, "Why does the girl fight the demons? Does she want their power so she can do evil herself, or does she want to make the world a kinder place?" Does Sadira embody the ideal demon hunter?

Why do you think the chalked image of a smiling face upsets Pargol so much?

Farrin wonders how Principal Kobra could ever know anything about demons. The principal does seem unsympathetic and hard. But how have her experiences shaped her character? Does she change as the story progresses?

Why do you think Farrin is so attracted to ghost stories, authors like Edgar Allen Poe, and television shows like *Kolchak: The Night Stalker*?

As much as Farrin dislikes her mother and the values her parents embrace, what traits from each parent does she unknowingly embody?

To Farrin, her parents' bombing parties seem the ultimate expression of frivolousness. How much does her parents' reaction to an uncertain future differ from Farrin and Sadira's?

Sadira says of the deaths in her family, "Most of the time, I think of it as a story that happened to someone else. Then I don't really feel it." Consider how Sadira, her father, Pargol, Principal Kobra, and ultimately Farrin herself deal with loss.

What is it about the moon that makes it a perfect symbol of Farrin and Sadira's relationship? By the end of the story, how does the moon take on additional meaning for Farrin?

When the girls perform the faal-e Hafez, the passage they point to is: *No death invades a heart that comes alive in love / Our immortality is etched in the book of life.* Sadira and Farrin find nothing but beauty in the words. How do you think they interpret this as a prediction of their future together?

When Pargol informs on the girls and the principal calls their parents, Farrin's reaction at the meeting is very different from Sadira's. Considering their backgrounds and the differences in their characters, what do you think Sadira's reaction signifies?

Farrin and Sadira are prepared to risk everything they have known, everything that keeps them safe, in order to be together. What is it about the power of love that sometimes makes us act in a way that is against our own best interests? How does logic drive Farrin? How much is she driven by emotion?

Power, or the lack of it, seems to bring out the worst in both Farrin and Ahmad. How much do you think culture dictates the way they relate to each other? How much does wealth play a role in their shifting relationship?

The author writes that being gay or lesbian is currently a criminal offence in more than seventy countries. And homosexuals face the death penalty in seven countries. At a time when gay rights have finally made some progress in the West, why do you think other countries have lagged behind so significantly?